J. T. EDSON'S
FLOATING OUTFIT

The toughest bunch of Rebels that ever lost a war, they fought for the South, and then for Texas, as the legendary Floating Outfit of "Ole Devil" Hardin's O.D. Connected ranch.

MARK COUNTER was the best-dressed man in the West: always dressed fit-to-kill. **THE YSABEL KID** was Comanche fast and Texas tough. And the most famous of them all was **DUSTY FOG**, the ex-cavalryman known as the Rio Hondo Gun Wizard.

J. T. Edson has captured all the excitement and adventure of the raw frontier in this magnificent Western series. Turn the page for a complete list of Berkley Floating Outfit titles.

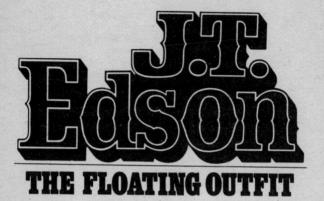

J.T. Edson

THE FLOATING OUTFIT

BERKLEY BOOKS, NEW YORK

Originally printed in Great Britain by
Brown Watson Limited.

This Berkley book contains the complete
text of the original edition.
It has been completely reset in a typeface
designed for easy reading, and was printed
from new film.

THE FLOATING OUTFIT

A Berkley Book/published by arrangement with
Transworld Publishers Ltd.

PRINTING HISTORY
Sabre edition published 1967
Berkley edition/September 1984

ISBN: 0-425-06999-0

A BERKLEY BOOK® TM 757,375
Berkley Books are published by The Berkley Publishing Group,
200 Madison Avenue, New York, New York 10016.
The name "BERKLEY" and the stylized "B" with design are
trademarks belonging to Berkley Publishing Corporation.
PRINTED IN THE UNITED STATES OF AMERICA

FOR MUM AND BILL

PART ONE

The Phantom of Gallup Creek

Wally Harris knew he was in for trouble as soon as he saw Stan Bialowski and Al Tupper enter his store. While the two big, heavily built men might wear the dress of cowhands, neither ever rode the range and worked at any task to do with handling cattle. At least they did not in the small Texas town of Gallup Creek. Employed as enforcers of Henry Claibourne's will, they found no time to perform the duties of cowhands; even if such work had ever been in their line. Bialowski and Tupper ensured that anybody who failed to comply with Claibourne's wishes rapidly regretted such an evil and foolish attitude.

Thinking back to the meeting of the previous night, Harris knew that he had transgressed and so stood a good chance of being a recipient of the two men's special attentions.

"Hear you been doing some talking, Wally," said Bialowski, leaning an elbow on the counter top and helping himself to a cigar from the box by the cash drawer.

"He's a real good talker," Tupper went on, dipping a hand into the candy jar and appropriating several lumps of its contents.

"I don't know what you mean," Harris stated, trying to sound unconcerned.

"Word has it that you've been saying that the Rangers should be brought in here," Bialowski explained. "Now why'd you say that, Wally?"

"You'll go and give Gallup Creek a bad name," Tupper went on, stuffing a piece of candy into his mouth. "Maybe even make folks think there's something dishonest going on hereabouts."

"And there isn't Wally," Bialowski purred, rasping a match on the counter top. "Now is there?"

No coward, Harris still knew the value of caution and discretion. Despite their amiable manner, the two men exuded menace to anyone who knew them. Clearly they knew of the secret meeting held by certain businessmen the previous night and possessed details of the matter discussed. Which meant that Harris stood a good chance of receiving a lesson to teach him the error of his ways. Yet the storekeeper knew something must be done. He felt that he could no longer stand back while a good share of his profits passed into the pockets of Henry Claibourne, the smooth-talking but deadly mayor of Gallup Creek. Owner of the Rocking Horse Saloon in addition to his civic office, Claibourne held Gallup Creek in the palms of his hands and milked it as effectively as a dirt-busting farmer cleared the udders of a cow.

Small Gallup Creek might be, but it stood in a position to catch trade from north-bound trail herds, supplied the needs of several good-sized ranches and offered a convenient point through which east-west traffic passed. Such a location ought to enrich its businessmen, or at least supply them with a reasonably affluent standard of living. So it did before the arrival of Henry Claibourne. On his arrival, Claibourne bought the Rocking Horse Saloon. Backed by a hard-case bunch, Claibourne elected himself mayor and set Jack Cable, a real fast man with a gun, in office as town marshal. Next he announced the collection of various taxes to be used on civic improvements and his lawmen saw to collecting the money demanded; although the promised improvements never made an appearance. Every business in town paid, or its owner pretty soon came to wish that he had. In addition to the saloon, Claibourne owned the livery barn, the local freight outfit, controlled the post-office and held the Wells Fargo agent's contract. Anybody who objected to his taxes could not ship in supplies, or send a request for an outside agency to bring them in; while also living in danger of physical injury to add to his troubles.

The meeting the previous evening, supposedly in secret, had been to discuss ways and means of ending Claibourne's reign as town boss. At it Harris spoke more than the others, suggesting that they went over the head of the local law and sent a request for assistance to the Texas Rangers. Although, at the time, that had seemed like a good idea, Harris now wondered if he might not have been wiser to have shown discretion. Maybe he ought to have kept quiet and used other means of bringing the Rangers to Gallup Creek. From the presence of Claibourne's men, he concluded he should have done so.

"What're you wanting?" he asked.

"You know what we want," answered Bialowski and dropped the lit match into the cigar box. He shot out his hand to catch Harris's wrist and prevented the storekeeper from dousing the flame which licked at the cigars. "From right now you keep your mouth shut about the running of this town."

Jerking his hand free from Bialowski's grasp, Harris put out the match but not before it had ruined several of the cigars. Anger glowed on the storekeeper's face, yet he knew he could accomplish nothing against the two men.

"You'd best listen, Wally," Tupper continued, shoving the candy jar from the counter with enough force to shatter it and spew its contents over the sawdust covered floor. "Mayor Claibourne don't take to citizens trying to make fuss for him."

"Which same, was he a mean cuss, he might double your taxes and have to put up your freight costs," Bialowski warned. "Fact being, he told us to collect a hundred dollars for improving your sidewalk. It's dangerous and some good citizen might bust a leg walking along it."

"A hundred—!" Harris gasped.

"It could be worse," grinned Tupper. "You've still got your health to help you earn more."

"Sure you have," agreed Bialowski. "Where's the hundred, Wally?"

"I don't have that much on hand right now," Harris replied.

"Then you'd best get it," growled Bialowski, all pretence falling aside. "There's no hurry—have it at the boss's office by sundown."

With that the two men turned and walked from the room. Slowly Harris raised his hand to wipe his brow and his eyes went to the spilled candy. Almost every piece had a coating of sawdust and would be unfit for sale. Anger filled him and he looked at the revolver under the counter. Shooting the two men might give him some small satisfaction, but that would not last long. Marshal Cable could then kill him, pretending that he resisted arrest, and Claibourne would take over his store in default of taxes.

Somehow or other Harris knew he must get help. Yet where could he find men willing to go against Claibourne's hired hard-cases? Certainly not in Gallup Creek, for the citizens had seen too many examples of what happened to men who opposed the town boss. If, however, he slipped out of town, he could ride over to Bentley City and use their telegraph to send for the Rangers.

A good idea, but one filled with difficulties. Bentley lay some eighty miles to the northwest and, although connected by a well-defined stagecoach trail, a long distance for a town-dweller to cover at speed on horseback. Yet it must be done at speed. Once Claibourne missed Harris, he would send men to bring the storekeeper back. Even leaving Gallup Creek presented a problem. While Harris owned a horse, he stabled it in the livery barn; the owner of which worked for Claibourne. Nor would Harris's gentle, leisurely harness-horse be suitable to make the hard, fast run to Bentley.

Despite being a middle-sized, amiable man running to soft plumpness, Harris had a shrewd brain and knew better than to take such a serious action without planning to increase his chances of success. Taking up a broom, he began to sweep the broken glass and scattered candy into a pile. As he worked he thought out a course of action and started to put it into being.

After locking up the front door, Harris emptied the cash drawer and put the money into his pocket. While he could not take a chance on withdrawing his bank account, he decided that it would be safe until his return with the Rangers. Throwing a final glance around the room, he left and drew open the rear door. Apparently Claibourne did not expect Harris to make any such sudden moves, for nobody watched the rear of the building. Harris turned the key in the back door and hurried along the back streets in the direction of the livery barn. Luck appeared to be favoring the storekeeper, for a finely built horse stood saddled and tied by its reins to a post by the barn's rear door. Moving forward, with darting glances about him, Harris began to unfasten the reins and while doing so heard the barn's door opening. Apprehension, mingled with fear, filled Harris. If one of Claibourne's men caught him, it would be the end of everything including his life. While one of the town boss's employees emerged from the barn, Harris felt a wave of relief. Short, bald, with a mean-looking face, the man was Gosling, owner of the barn, not one of the hard-cases. A look of surprise came to Gosling's face at finding Harris.

"Hey!" the barn owner yelped. "What's th—"

At which point Harris hit Gosling as hard as he could. Considering that the storekeeper did not indulge in brawls and had not raised his hand against another person since his early youth, he achieved a pretty fair result. Gosling's head snapped back under the impact of Harris's knuckles. Spun around by the force of the blow, the barn's owner crashed head-first into the wall, groaned and slid down.

For a moment Harris stood staring down at the other man, then a spirit of self-preservation took hold of him. Up until that moment he might have been free to return to the store, pay his fine and continue existing as before. From the moment his fist landed that all changed. If he hoped to survive with his life, he must mount the horse and ride.

Working as quickly as his fumbling fingers would allow, Harris unfastened the horse. It moved restlessly and caused him to grab hurriedly at it. However he managed to mount and felt the quiver of a more powerful body than he normally used between his legs. However the horse had been well enough trained to make no fuss and on being started moving strode out at a good pace away from the town.

Holding the horse to a fast trot, Harris made a circle beyond the edge of Gallup Creek and joined the Bentley trail about a mile outside the town. With a well-defined route to follow, the storekeeper made better time for the earth of the trail made for ease of traveling when astride a good horse. Normally when on a long journey he would have traveled by stage-coach, or in his buckboard and soon learned the difference between that mode of transport and sitting the back of a fast-striding horse. However he gritted his teeth and clung on, determined not to be captured by Claibourne's men.

After a couple of hours' traveling, Harris slowed the horse up. While not over-experienced in such matters, he figured that it might be best not to push the willing animal too hard in case he needed to gallop later when his pursuers made their presence known. Turning as best he could in the saddle, he scanned the back trail, but saw nothing and was compelled to give his full attention to the horse before he could make a real careful examination.

Six miles from Gallup Creek the trail wound down a long slope, through wooded country until it reached the Bass Creek of the Brazos River. Just as Harris came into sight of the ford by which stage-coaches crossed the wide, shallow stream, he became aware that a man stood allowing a big paint horse to drink before riding over to his side. The fear which rose in Harris had begun to die down with the realization that the man was a stranger, when the storekeeper heard a vicious "splat!" sound by his right ear. Never having been shot at before, Harris failed to recognize the sound of a close-passing bullet.

Not so the man on the opposite bank. On hearing Harris's approaching horse, he looked in the storekeeper's direction. Apparently satisfied that there would be no danger, the man resumed watching his paint drinking. When the bullet drove by him, he shot out his hand to slide the Winchester Model 1873 carbine from its saddleboot. Moving at a speed which made Harris blink, the man dropped his right knee to the sand at the stream's edge, whipped the carbine to his shoulder, sighted along its barrel and fired in what appeared to be one continuous flow of action.

A scream, chilling in its intensity, rang out from on the slope above Harris, followed by a thrashing sound among the bushes. Swinging astride his horse, the man threw another bullet into the carbine's breech and rode forward. Shocked by the sudden action, and fully occupied with trying to control his equally startled mount, Harris did no more than stare as the man rode by him. Fortunately for the storekeeper, the horse he acquired in Gallup Creek was too tired to make a hard struggle. However by the time he regained control of his mount, he heard the other man coming back down the slope and turned to face him.

"That feller up there," the man said, resting the carbine on his knees. "He's wearing a deputy marshal's badge. I reckon we'd best have a talk—don't you?"

Towards noon on the day after Harris's flight from Gallup Creek, a small cowhand rode into town from the opposite side to the Bentley trail. All in all, he did not make an imposing sight. He sat just about the most sorry specimen of a horse either Bialowski or Tupper had ever seen. Standing on the porch of the Rocking Horse Saloon, they studied the newcomer without any great interest. At most he would not top five foot six, with a handsome face and dusty blond hair which showed from under the brim of a woolsey copy of a Stetson hat two sizes too large for him. His clothing had the appearance of being cast-offs, patched and a poor fit, while his boots had scuffed and worn-down heels. Around his waist hung a gunbelt with a battered old Navy Colt riding in a holster far too high for a fast draw and which permitted only its butt to show above the thick, stiff leather. Taken with the horse, that looked like a cull from a poor quality ranch, a beat-up saddle, torn tarp around a small bundle on the cantle and cheap rope at the horn, the rider looked neither impressive nor dangerous.

"Now ain't they just about the sorriest sight you ever did see, Stan?" asked Tupper with a grin.

"He's sure a tophand from some outfit," chuckled Bialowski. "And that hoss there'd take prizes any place."

If the young man heard the words, he gave no sign of it. Swinging the horse to a halt before the saloon's hitching rail, he tossed his leg over the saddle in what ought to have been a flashy dismount if he had not stumbled and almost fallen when he landed on the ground.

"You finding something funny?" he asked the two men as they howled with laughter.

"Who us?" Bialowski replied. "Why no. Say, do that there fancy get-off again, we didn't see it right first time."

"Sure don't know how he could take such a chance, that being a real mean hoss," Tupper went on. "I bet it'd run like a Neuces steer happen you poked it up the rump with a cigar."

"Which same I've got the cigar to try," Bialowski stated and the men swung from the porch.

"You keep away from my hoss," warned the newcomer.

"My! Ain't he the fiesty one!" Bialowski grinned and advanced, sucking at his cigar to make its end glow red.

Seeing that the hard-case intended to ram the hot cigar against the rump of his horse, the youngster knocked Bialowski's hand aside and whipped across a punch at the man. It seemed that the newcomer knew little or nothing about fist-fighting for the blow came in an awkward, telegraphed manner which Bialowski found no difficulty in handling. Casually Bialowski slapped the youngster's punch aside, laid a hand against his face and thrust him back into Tupper's arms. Born bullies, the two men liked nothing better than the situation they found themselves in. Rough-handling the young cowhand would make a break from the monotony and both decided to enjoy it to the full.

Throwing a powerful forearm around the youngster, Tupper slid the Navy Colt from its holster; although not without difficulty, for the leather clung to it. An idea formed in his head and he propelled the youngster back to Bialowski with a thrust of his knee. Enfolding the youngster in his arms and controlling his struggles with no difficulty, Bialowski turned him so that he could not see what Tupper did to the revolver.

"Let me go, damn you!" yelled the cowhand, trying without success to pull free from Bialowski's hands. "Give me back my gun, you lousy skunks."

With a grin, Tupper stepped forward and thrust the revolver down hard into the holster. "Turn him loose, Stan," he said.

Bialowski released the youngster and thrust him contemptuously away. Catching his balance, the cowhand swung to face his tormentors and his hand lifted over the revolver's butt. Anger and humiliation flushed his cheeks as he faced the mocking pair.

"Go ahead, curly wolf," Bialowski grinned. "Make your move."

"Damn it, I will!" the youngster yelled back. "Nobody treats Dave Cleat like that and gets away with it."

"Damned if he ain't fixing to take us both, Stan," Tupper grinned.

"It sure looks that way, Al," Bialowski replied.

"Draw, damn you!" Dave Cleat howled and grabbed at his gun's butt.

With the holster riding so high and badly constructed, a considerable pull was required to draw the Colt. Nor did the young cowboy show any great skill in the matter. His hand closed and he tugged hard at the butt. Out slid the Colt, or a part of it. While its owner had been prevented from watching him, Tupper forced out the wedge which held the lock frame and barrel of the gun together. So when Dave Cleat tugged at the butt, he brought out the lock frame and cylinder but left the barrel in the holster. While the Colt might still have fired without its barrel assembly, the cylinder was dragged down its spindle far enough to prevent the hammer striking the percussion caps on the nipples.

"It looks like you got trouble, curly wolf," grinned Tupper.

"I sure never saw a gun like that afore," Bialowski went on.

Giving a yell of frustrated fury, Cleat flung himself at his tormentors and swung up the useless portion of the gun. Bialowski backhanded him savagely across the face and Tupper ripped a punch into his middle. Gasping, gagging and doubled over, Dave Cleat stumbled away, fell against the hitching rail and sank to his knees on the ground. Even as the two men moved towards Cleat, a small, pretty girl in a plain black dress ran between them. Fury showed on her face as she glared at the pair of hard-cases.

"You great hulking brutes!" she gasped. "Keep away from him."

Just what effect Mary Hocknell's intervention might have had was never put to the test. Marshal Jack Cable came around the corner of the saloon and walked towards the batwing doors of the main entrance. Tall, slim, he dressed far too well for the marshal on a small town's salary to account for his sartorial taste. A costly white Stetson rode his pomaded hair. In some circles he might have been termed handsome, with a neat moustache and long side-burns of the latest Eastern fashion. He went in for cutaway coats, fancy shirts and vests, string ties, town pants and walking boots, but the gun belt around his waist spelled pure West and its contoured holster carried an ivory-handled .44 caliber Remington 1875 Army revolver just right for a rapid withdrawal.

"Inside, you pair," he said, expressing no surprise at finding two of his men assaulting a stranger in the street.

Obediently Bialowski and Tupper followed the marshal into the saloon and Mary knelt at Dave Cleat's side. Concern showed on the girl's pretty face as she looked at the young man.

"Are you badly hurt?" she asked.

Lifting his face, the cowhand shook his head. "I—I'll do," he gasped.

"Let me help you up," the girl went on, then saw her father approaching although nobody else offered to come over. "Papa, this young man was attacked by two of Claibourne's men."

"So I saw," said the Reverend Maurice Hocknell grimly. "I came as soon as I saw what was happening."

"You couldn't have stopped it," Mary said bitterly.

"Let me help you, son," Hocknell offered.

A look of surprise flickered across the preacher's face as he took hold of the cowhand's arm, meaning to assist the other to his feet. However he held down any comment he might have wished to make, after taking a quick glance at the front of the saloon. Helping Dave Cleat to stand erect, Hocknell led him across the street and Mary showed a practical turn of mind by taking the sorry-looking horse's reins then leading the animal after the two men.

In the saloon Cable led the way to a door marked "Private", knocked and entered. Rising from behind the desk, Henry Claibourne threw a glance at the two hard-cases and then gave his attention to the marshal. Big, running to fat, well-dressed and jovial-looking, the town boss's eyes and rat-trap mouth alone gave a true hint of his character.

"Joe's not back yet," Cable said.

"Maybe he hasn't caught up with Harris," Claibourne replied. "That was a good horse he took."

"Yeah," growled Cable. "I know. It was mine."

"Could be that Joe didn't get to Harris before they hit Bentley," Claibourne said, ignoring the interruption. "He knows what to do in that case."

"You ought to have let me and some more of the boys go along," the marshal stated.

"And I told you why I didn't," answered Claibourne. "There are around a hundred men in this town. I only hire nine. But as long as the townies don't join together that's enough. So I wanted as many of you as possible here to act as a reminder, a show of force."

"Hell, boss," Bialowski put in, "we've got this town buffaloed."

"Sure we have," agreed Claibourne, "And for why? Because we're organized and they're not. If they ever get organized, we're in bad trouble."

"It'll never happen," scoffed Tupper.

"It *can* happen!" warned Claibourne. "All they need is a leader."

"Which they won't find in this town," Cable sneered. "Look at that meeting they called last night. Weren't but a handful of townies turned up and one of them come running straight to you with word of what was said."

"Sure," admitted Claiborne. "But if they ever get a real fighting man as a leader—"

A frantic banging at the rear door of the office chopped off Claibourne's words. Crossing the room, Cable unlocked and opened the door almost to be trampled under-foot as Gosling charged through. With his face ashy, scared-looking, the owner of the livery barn raised a shaking hand to point behind him.

"Ou—Out—th—there!"

Drawing his Remington, Cable lunged through the door. He did not know what to expect and the sight awaiting him brought him to a sudden halt. Hardened killer though he might be, Cable could not prevent himself taking a hurried step to the rear, or hold down a nervous gulp.

Draped across the saddle of a horse, left grotesquely stiff by *rigor mortis* setting in, the body of his deputy did not make a pleasant picture. After the initial shock wore off, Cable noticed a sheet of paper attached to the body's vest. He heard the startled exclamations of the other occupants of the room as they came outside but ignored them. Taking the sheet of paper, he drew it free, opened it and read the message on it.

"Hell fire!" he gasped, turning to Claibourne. "Take a look at this."

"To Claibourne and his hired hands," the message read, written neatly and by a hand which obviously used a pen often enough to keep in practice. *"You've robbed the folk of Gallup Creek for too long. Get out or take the consequences. Dusty Fog."*

After reading the contents of the paper, Claibourne turned a worried face towards the marshal. "Is it for real?"

"I don't know," Cable admitted, "not having ever seen Dusty Fog's writing."

Despite the attempt at levity, Cable sounded just a mite uneasy. Since the War Between The States—during it too for that matter—the name of Dusty Fog had gone far across the Western range country. As a Confederate cavalry captain at only seventeen, he gained a reputation as a military raider which many a professional soldier might have envied. With the coming of peace, Dusty Fog took over as segundo of the great OD Connected ranch; an outfit that claimed few peers in the matter of salty toughness. Twice he took over as lawman and tamed mighty rough towns to the full satisfaction of their law-abiding citizens.* In addition, folks spoke of him as a trail boss second to none, gave him credit for being well-able to handle his part in a rough-house brawl. Mostly, though, they told of his almost uncanny wizardry in the use of a matched brace of Colt Civilian Model Peacemakers. Even among the top names of the fast-draw breed, many acknowledged—if grudgingly and only to themselves—that Dusty Fog was fastest and most accurate of them all.

More than that, Dusty Fog did not ride alone when he went to war. With him came four men each almost as deadly efficient as himself. Formed originally as the elite of the OD Connected's crew to act as a floating outfit, a mobile group who covered the ranch's furthest ranges instead of being based at the main house, the quartet more and more came to work as trouble-shooters for Ole Devil Hardin. When a friend of the rancher found himself in a dangerous position and asked for help, the floating outfit supplied it and they had proven remarkably adept at doing so. More than one hard-case, wild onion crew learned to sing soft and gentle when Dusty Fog and his four companions appeared on the scene.

Small wonder then that Claibourne looked worried when he read the note. He might have nine men to back his play, but they seemed like mighty short odds when stacked up against the combined talents of Ole Devil's floating outfit.

"Do you reckon he could have wrote it?" Claibourne insisted.

"Damned if I know, and that's for sure," Cable replied. "Why'd he be worried about something that happens here? We're a long ways from the Rio Hondo and as far as I know

*Told in *Quiet Town* and *The Trouble Busters*.

we've never done a thing to him."

"What's up, boss?" Bialowski asked.

"Read this," Claibourne answered and passed over the paper. When the hard-case finished reading, the town boss went on, "have you seen any strangers come into town?"

"Only that short-growed runt just now, and he for sure wasn't Dusty Fog."

"How do you know?" Claibourne asked.

"Have you seen Dusty Fog?" Cable continued.

"No," admitted Bialowski, "But I've seen that kid who just come in. He's a short runt, like I said, not more'n five foot six at most, afork the worse cull of a crowbait I've ever seen."

"Me 'n' Stan took his gun off him," Tupper told Claibourne. "An old Navy Colt so rusted that the bullets'd have to dig their way out of the barrel. He sure didn't stack too high when we rough-handled him some, either."

"One thing I do know," said Bialowski. "If *he's* Dusty Fog, he don't scare me none at all."

"Way I hear it," Cable remarked, "Fog's a real big jasper. Six foot three at least and as strong as a hoss. He must be. I met up with one of the fellers who saw him half-kill Sandra Howkins's brother and two of her men with his bare hands."*

"Which same that kid we just saw can't be him," stated Bialowski. "Way he handled himself, he couldn't hit his way through a sheet of wet paper."

Dismissing the new arrival as a possibility, due to his men's comments, Claibourne looked at the body across the saddle and a thought struck him.

"Gosling," he said. "Who knows about this?"

"Nobody that I know of," Gosling answered. "I saw the hoss coming across the range towards my place and off the

---

*Told in *A Town Called Yellowdog*.

Bentley trail and fetched it straight over here."

"Did you see anybody with it?"

"Nope. It come in alone."

Any range-bred horse would return to its home once it found itself free and the dead deputy had resided for long enough in Gallup Creek to make his mount regard the livery barn in that light.

"What I don't see," Cable put in, "is why Dusty Fog'd pull a game like this."

"How do you mean?" asked Claibourne.

"Sending Joe's body in with a message. Happen he aimed to take cards, why didn't him and the rest of the floating outfit just ride in. They'd've been among us afore we knew anything was wrong."

"There's that to it," admitted Claibourne.

"Maybe Harris killed Joe and did it to throw a scare into us," Bialowski suggested. "Although I wouldn't expect him to have the guts to do it."

"A scared man'll do things he wouldn't any other time," Gosling pointed out.

"A stunt like this's not the work of a scared man," growled Claibourne.

"Then Dusty Fog might've done it," Gosling whispered, casting a nervous glance around him.

"Or somebody smart might be blaming him for it," answered Claibourne. "If that horse'd've come into town along Main Street folks would have seen it. Some of them would have read the note. Figuring a man like Dusty Fog's backing them could give them the courage to stand against us."

"What'll we do then, boss?" Bialowski inquired.

"You and Tupper can see to getting Joe out of sight."

"We'll take him to the undertake—"

"The hell you will!" Claibourne interrupted. "You pair bury him on the range and make sure nobody sees you do it. I don't want any of the townies to know about this business."

"I've got shovels and a pick at the barn," Gosling put in and almost immediately regretted the offer.

"Then you can come and help us use 'em," snorted Bialowski. "You found Joe, so you can help plant him."

Although the barn's owner might have liked to argue the point, Claibourne growled an order to him and he went along with the two hard-cases. Cable watched the men depart and then turned to the town boss.

"I don't like it," the marshal stated.

"Or me," admitted Claibourne. "Seeing Joe across that saddle handed me a hell of a shock too. And that was just what it was meant to do. Let's go back inside, Jack."

On re-entering the office, Cable went to the desk, took out a bottle and glasses, then poured out two drinks. "I don't like it," he stated again.

"Or me," repeated Claibourne. "But is Dusty Fog behind it, or is it one of the townies playing smart?"

"If I thought that—" Cable began.

"We'll play it that Fog's behind it," Claibourne decided. "If he had the full floating outfit behind him, he'd just come into town and handle things in a straightforward way."

"Yeah," breathed Cable. "But if he was alone, he might pull something like this."

"Do you reckon you can take him if he comes?"

"I never yet met the man I couldn't."

"Then all we have to do is wait and watch for Fog to come. A feller like him will be hard to miss. Just to make sure, though, you'd best have two of the boys making the rounds all night. If it's Fog, they'll likely see him. And if it's only some townie playing smart, it won't do any harm to show them that we're ready for trouble."

"I'll see to it," promised Cable.

* * *

That night Bialowski and Tupper slouched slowly side by side along the sidewalk before the saddler's shop which stood next to the Wells Fargo office building, although separated from it by a wide alley. Neither of the men had relished the task of patrolling the streets after midnight, but a few drinks gave them what passed for courage and at first, made the business less unpleasant. Filled with whisky-inspired bravado at first, they paraded the streets and made many loud comments as to the fate of Dusty Fog should he appear. However, with the time approaching three in the morning much of their ardor had died down.

"This is a lousy, no good chore," Bialowski declared for at least the tenth time. "Two of us can't cover the whole of the town."

"Fog wouldn't come in at this time of the night anyways," Tupper answered, walking on the inside and passing the end of the building. "He'd—"

Before the hard-case could continue with his views on the matter, he felt a powerful hand clamp hold of his arm. Then he was jerked into the blackness of the alley and swung around. Even as he thought of yelling a warning, something smashed into his throat with savage force. Tupper did not know what hit him, except that it felt like the blunt end of an axe's head. What he did know was that it hurt like hell, chopped off his breath, prevented him from shouting and sent him stumbling back with open mouth working in soundless agony.

For a moment Bialowski just stood and stared, taken completely by surprise when Tupper shot from his side and into the alley. Then he heard the thud of the blow and made out the shape of his companion's attacker, a black form darker than the surrounding blackness of the alley. With a low snarl, Bialowski charged forward and saw the attacker turn towards him. His hands missed the other man and he felt his vest gripped then pulled. Losing his balance, he gave a startled yelp. A foot rammed into his belly as the attacker collapsed under him, then the world seemed to spin around. For a moment Bialowski's body left the ground, but came back to it in no uncertain manner. He lit down on his back, landing hard and with all the wind jarred from his body by the impact.

Still choking, Tupper staggered forward. He had been out in the night long enough to be able to see fairly well and made out the shape of the attacker. After throwing Bialowski in that spectacular manner, the attacker rolled over on to his belly and started to rise. Tupper sprang forward and launched a kick, aiming it at the other's head. Pain slowed him and he felt two hands clamp hold of his ankle. Rising, the attacker gave the trapped ankle a twisting heave which threw Tupper across the alley to crash into the raised wooden platform erected outside the Wells Fargo office to aid the loading and unloading of freight.

A few kegs stood on the platform, having been left there by the Wells Fargo agent ready for loading on to a wagon the following morning, but Tupper ignored them. Twisting to face the attacker, he reached for his gun. Already the attacker approached, coming in fast. Tupper could not form a clear idea of what the attacker might be like, or even what kind of build the other possessed, being more concerned with his troubles. Before he reached any conclusions, or managed to draw the gun, Tupper formed a vague impression that the attacker bounded into the air. Then a boot smashed into his forehead, ripping open the skin and blood ran down half-blinding him. Dazed by the kick, Tupper fell back against the platform again. He clutched at his forehead, twisting in an attempt to avoid further punishment, and stumbled away.

By that time Bialowski had recovered enough to sit up. Taking in the situation, the hard-case rose and, as the attacker landed from delivering that leaping kick to Tupper, reached towards his thigh. His hand struck an empty holster. While making the involuntary somersault, Bialowski's Colt had slipped from his holster and lay somewhere on the floor of the alley. Snarling his fury, he hurled himself at the attacker and his big hands reached out ready to grip the other.

On landing, the attacker pivoted around to meet the new danger and handled it as effectively as the other attempts. His right hand caught Bialowski's left wrist from underneath, forcing it outwards. Across came the attacker's left hand to grip the trapped wrist from above, while his feet started to swing his body to the right. In doing so, he turned the palm of Bialowski's hand upwards in an awkward manner. Continuing his turn, the attacker bent his knees slightly and carried the captured arm upwards then over his own head. So smoothly and swiftly did he act that he gave Bialowski no chance of countering the attack. Pressing downwards on the wrist again, the attacker gave Bialowski no choice but be thrown over. Once more the burly hard-case's feet left the ground, only this time he did not land so luckily. On the way down his rump smashed into the platform with shattering violence. A scream burst from his lips, then his head struck the ground and he collapsed into black unconsciousness.

A shot roared, sounding like a thunder-clap in the confines of the alley, and the bullet narrowly missed the attacker's head. Swinging around, the attacker saw Tupper moving closer and guessed that the hard-case had called off fighting with bare hands. So he had. Tupper wanted no part of the attacker, having tasted the other's very effective methods. Unlike Bialowski, Tupper still wore his gun. However, dazed and half-blind from his own blood, the hard-case made the mistake of missing his shot. Seeing that, he started to move into a range where such would be all but impossible.

Springing to the platform, the attacker caught up one of the kegs. He felt its weight as he turned towards his assailant, hoisted it upwards and hurled it straight at the advancing hard-case. In his dazed condition Tupper failed to see the danger until too late. Full into his chest crashed the heavy keg, halting his advance. A shriek of agony left him as he pitched over backwards. Knocked aside, his revolver fired again and its bullet went harmlessly into the wall of the Wells Fargo building. Then Tupper went down and the keg rolled from his body.

Already the noise attracted attention. Bedroom windows jerked up, lights glowed and voices shouted meaningless questions. Feet thudded as Cable and three of his men left the jail-house at a run. Guns in hand, one of them also carried a lantern, the quartet headed along the street in the direction of the alley. The attacker threw a quick glance around him, then bounded off into the darkness at the rear of the building.

"Up here!" Cable barked a moment later, skidding to a halt as he heard a low groaning from the alley.

Entering the alley, Cable's party came to a halt and stared at the scene illuminated by the lantern's glow. Bialowski sprawled motionless on the ground by the platform ahead of them and further along lay the writhing, moaning form of Tupper. At the second hard-case's side, a keg lay spewing out nails from its burst-open top.

"What the hell—!" began the man with the lantern.

"Come on!" Cable yelled, realizing that whoever left the two hard-cases in that condition must have gone the rear way.

Showing caution, the quartet moved through the alley.

Although they halted at the rear, no sound came to help them decide which way the attacker went. All realized that they presented him with a good target happen he wanted to start shooting and Cable gave the order to move back into the alley once more. Returning to their injured companions, the men looked down and the one carrying the lantern knelt at Tupper's side.

"Who the hell did this?" he asked, looking up at the others after examining the injuries. "His chest's damned near caved in."

"So your'n'd be happen you'd been hit with that keg," Cable answered. "Get Doc Smith here, *pronto*."

Like a number of citizens, the town's doctor had heard the shooting. He came hurriedly, carrying his medical bag, for gun-fire at that hour of the morning usually meant he would have work to do. After looking at Bialowski, the doctor rose and walked towards Tupper. In passing, he asked Cable a question.

"How'd this happen?"

Which thought had been running through the marshal's mind and leaving him heartily disliking any of the obvious conclusions. All too well Cable knew the two men's ability in the fighting line and their injuries proved that at last they had met more than their match. Even accepting that they had fallen victims of a surprise attack, it seemed unlikely that Bialowski and Tupper could both have been put out of action quick enough to prevent them giving a good account of themselves.

Had it been an assault by a group of men?

Before the marshal could make any decision on that point, the doctor rose from Tupper's side and asked for help to take the two men to his office.

"Bialowski's got a busted head, but his back's not broke," Cable reported to Claibourne, after seeing his injured men carried off. "Which same he was lucky. Al Tupper wasn't. The Doc stitched his head up and reckons he's got three bust ribs."

"You've no idea who did it?"

"None. The ground in that alley's too hard to show sign. Whoever did it must be damned strong. He heaved a forty pound keg of nails a fair distance to hit Tupper and that took strength."

"How about that feller who came in yesterday?" asked Claibourne. "If those two worked him over, he'd have a hate against them."

"Sure," admitted Cable. "But I saw him and you didn't. A short-growed runt like him couldn't've took Bialowski or Tupper, much less both of them together."

"How about a bunch of the townies having done it?"

"I wondered about that and threw it out," the marshal answered. "You know those two. They mightn't have had a brain between them, but they were tough. And happen a bunch'd jumped them, they'd've got their guns working sooner."

"You're not saying that one man jumped them?"

"I'm trying not to even *think* it. What one man could handle two big yahoos like that pair?"

"Dusty Fog was supposed to have took on three men."

"I've been thinking about that, too," said Cable. "What do you want me to do now, Henry?"

"There's not much you can do before morning," Claibourne replied. "Keep all the men out until daylight. Half around the saloon and the rest watching the town. Comes daylight, we'll see what we can learn."

A shock greeted Cable as he walked from the jail to the saloon at half past eight in the morning. While his men had reluctantly patrolled the streets, they appeared to have made a poor job of it. Pinned to the wall by the batwing doors of the saloon hung a sheet of paper. Already a trio of townsmen stood reading the message on it and they withdrew hurriedly as Cable approached. He halted, looked at the paper, snarled and cursed and tore it down. Yet he knew the damage had been done. The three townsmen would soon be spreading the word, repeating what they had read, telling their friends.

"Take warning, Claibourne," read Cable. "I aim to run you and all your bunch out of town. The two last night should show you that I mean business. Dusty Fog."

Just as Cable turned to enter the saloon, he saw Mary Hocknell and the young cowhand leave the preacher's house and come walking along the street. Crossing over, the marshal looked long and hard at the young man. While Dave Cleat seemed to be well built for his size, it hardly appeared likely that he could attack and beat Bialowski and Tupper.

"How come you're still in town, feller?" the marshal asked.

"My hoss's tuckered out," Dave Cleat replied. "So the parson let me stay on for a spell."

"Is your pappy taking in saddle-tramps now, Miss Hocknell?" Cable said.

"David is no saddle-tramp," the girl answered hotly. "He's looking for work in town right now. And those bullies attacked him yesterday—"

"He shouldn't have given them any lip," Cable interrupted, but an idea formed and he started to put it into practice. "If he wants work, I reckon I can help him. Come down to the Wells Fargo office, the agent wants a swamper and I'll ask him to take you on."

"Gee, thanks marshal," Dave Cleat said eagerly. "Did those fellers get hurt bad last night?"

"Bad enough. Where was you?"

"In bed. I heard the shooting, but one thing I learned is to stay well clear of gun-play."

"Where'd you work afore you come here?" asked Cable as he walked with the girl and cowhand towards the Wells Fargo office.

"Down south a few places. Say, was it Dusty Fog who downed your men?"

"Why'd you ask?" growled Cable.

"I saw him yesterday," Dave replied.

"You saw him?" repeated the marshal.

"Sure. I worked in John County for a spell and he used to come into Diggers Wells. There's a man you'd never forget. Six foot three, shoulders as wide as a set of batwing doors. I'd know him anywhere."

"Where'd you see him?"

"On the Sibley trail. He come on to it from back of town here."

All the time Dave Cleat spoke, Cable watched his face. The young man appeared to be telling the truth, for he met the marshal's eyes without flinching. A cold feeling ran through Cable and he glanced around him quickly. If Dusty Fog had released the dead deputy's horse, he would have just about reached the trail around the time Dave Cleat rode towards Gallup Creek.

"Did he say anything?" growled Cable.

"Nope. Just rode by and kept going."

Which meant little as he could find numerous places in which to hide. Before Cable could say any more, they reached the Wells Fargo office. Telling Dave Cleat to wait outside, Cable entered and gave the agent instructions. Then the marshal returned to where Dave waited.

"You're hired," he said. "The agent wants you to go round and make a start by toting those kegs into the office for him."

"I'll see you at lunch-time, David," Mary said and walked away.

Watched by the marshal and the agent, who came out of the office, Dave Cleat went around the building and stepped on to the loading platform. Bending, he tilted one of the kegs so that he could grip its bottom. With a grunt, the small cowhand lifted the keg from the ground and walked slowly into the office with it.

"It couldn't've been him," the agent said.

"Looks that way," Cable agreed. "But watch him careful—and watch out for a real big jasper wearing two white handled Colts too."

The day dragged slowly by, with Claibourne's men staying nervously on the alert. Word spread around the town, just as Claibourne and Cable guessed it would, and the citizens began to take heart at the thought that the finest gun-fighter in Texas being in the vicinity and backing them. When two of Claibourne's men returned to the saloon with word that the butcher refused to pay an overdue tax, the town boss knew he must make a move.

Backed by three men, Cable visited the butcher and pistol-whipped him once. A small crowd gathered and, while they made no move to intervene, showed such sullen anger that Cable did not chance forcing the issue. Instead he contented himself with warning the butcher that he would be coming for the money the following morning and aimed to get it one way or another. Despite putting on a brave front, the butcher felt worried, for he knew what the threat meant. Unless something happened before then, he would either have to pay or fight in the morning and he knew just how little chance he had in a shooting match against the marshal.

However both Claibourne and Cable had troubles of their own. When the town boss heard of his marshal's actions, he stated that the other ought to have acted in a more prudent manner.

"You said that we had to make him pay," Cable objected.

"So we do," Claibourne answered. "If he gets away with it, the town'll know we're running scared. Can we get any more men here?"

"Not within the next couple of days," replied Cable. "I could try telegraphing a couple of fellers I know who might be able to get us some, but it'll be days afore they arrive."

"Then we'll just have to do the best we can. Tomorrow morning I want you to take every man we've got and have a showdown with the butcher."

"And Dusty Fog?"

"If he's in town, or near at hand, he'll have to show himself then."

"Yeah," growled Cable. "And once he shows himself, I'll find out if he's as fast as everybody reckons."

Following the plans formulated with Claibourne, Cable ordered the saloon closed at ten o'clock. He then served notice that anybody seen on the streets after eleven would be shot and none of his audience doubted but he meant every word. In much less than the allowed hour, Gallup Creek resembled a ghost town. Only a trio of hard-cases moved on the streets. Armed with ten-gauge shotguns to augment their revolvers, the men kept to the center of the street and stayed close together as they paid particular attention to the alley mouths and other dark areas.

Cable knew that his men would shirk their duties unless kept under observation. So he and the res most reliable of the remaining men stayed in the jail building to supervize the others. Apart from the trio on patrol, every other available man waited in the saloon.

Midnight came and went at last the deputy rose to his feet. "I've got to go out back," he said.

"Watch what you're doing," warned Cable. "And keep your gun out."

"Trust me for that," replied the deputy and went into the rear of the building.

Before opening the rear door, the deputy drew his revolver. The rear of the jail had a compound surrounded by a ten foot high wooden fence and a backhouse stood in one corner. Cautiously the deputy advanced across the compound. However on reaching the backhouse's door he holstered his revolver. Hinges creaked as he drew open the door. Something swished through the air, coming from inside the backhouse and a heavy weight struck the deputy on the head. He collapsed without a sound and a man stepped from the building. Taking hold of the unconscious deputy, the man hauled him into the backhouse and sat him on the seat. With that done, the man crossed the compound and entered the jail.

"Anything doing out there?" Cable asked as the door behind him opened.

"Enough," replied a voice.

A soft, easy Texas drawl which most certainly did not come from the deputy who left the room to go out back. Turning, Cable looked at the man in the doorway and gave particular attention to the gunbelt with matched white-handled Colt Civilian Peacemakers butt forward in the contoured holsters.

"You!" the marshal snarled and grabbed at the Remington's butt.

Never had Cable moved with such deadly speed. Yet fast though his hand closed on the waiting gun's butt, he found himself too slow. In a flickering blur of movement almost too fast to be seen, the man in the doorway drew his Colts. While Cable's Remington still rose over the holster lip, the man's hands crossed, each brought out a gun, lining and firing the weapons. Half a second after he made his opening move, Cable felt lead tear into his body. Three men had died before his gun in Gallup Creek. Not one of them stood a chance against him, but he had finally met his match.

Even as the Remington clattered to the floor and Cable crashed backwards, the man in the doorway turned and went back the way he came.

Feet thudded on the street and across the sidewalk. The door of the office burst in and the patrolling trio entered with their shotguns held ready for use. For a moment they stood, staring around them, then the man in the center moved forward, placed a toe under Cable's shoulder and rolled the marshal over.

"He—He's dead!"

"Whoever did it went out of the back door," replied the medium-sized man at the right.

Advancing cautiously, the trio left the building and halted in the compound. While it looked empty and deserted, a slight noise drew their attention to the backhouse. Inside it the unconscious deputy could hardly have selected a worse time to recover. Although his movement had been involuntary, it made enough of a disturbance to reach the ears of the three men from the jail. To them it seemed that whoever was inside the backhouse had made the noise in moving surreptitiously and without intending that they should hear.

Three shotguns boomed loud, tearing the night's blackness apart with the red flare of the muzzle-blasts and shattering the silence. Nor did the men stop at merely firing the contents of one barrel. Instead each of them touched off first left then right trigger and a hail of fifty-four .32 caliber buckshot balls ripped into the backhouse's door. While a ten gauge shotgun might lack the long-range efficiency of

a Sharps Old Reliable buffalo rifle, up to a distance of fifty
yards or so it still drove its charge with sufficient force to
penetrate the planks of the small building and do considerable damage to anybody inside. All of the balls did not
strike the unconscious deputy, of course, for the charges
had spread apart during their flight. However enough struck
home to do their work.

Letting the now-empty shotguns fall from their hands,
the three men drew their revolvers and advanced toward the
backhouse. Before they arrived, its door inched open and
they prepared to shoot even though they knew that only a
miracle could have saved the man inside. Pushed open by
the weight leaning against it, the door continued to move
and the dead deputy slid into sight but landed face down.

"We got him!" whooped one of the trio. "Let's take a
look at his face."

Walking forward, the man rolled the body over and rasped
a match on his pants' seat. In its glow of illumination he
looked down at the agony distorted face. A startled gasp
left his lips and he flung the match aside as he rose hurriedly
to his feet.

"This here's Wade!" he announced in a voice that shook
with mixed emotions.

There had been no need for the words, his companions
saw as much as he did in the match's glowing light.

"Then the feller who killed Cable could be—" began the
medium-sized man; a tough and capable hired *pistolero*
called Jeavons. His words died away as their full import
struck him.

Nor did the other pair—using the names Freeman and
Todd in Gallup creek—need any fuller explanation. Like
Jeavons, they knew that the killer of Marshal Cable might
even now be watching them over the sights of a revolver
and hidden in the darkness. Having spent most of their

grown lives taking pay for fighting ability, the two men could sum up such a situation with ability and accuracy. Realizing the danger, they took steps to lessen it.

Turning fast, all three of the men dashed back to the office. Not until safely inside, with the door closed and locked, did any of them relax and only a little even then. Keeping clear of the windows and dousing all but one lamp, Jeavons looked at his companions.

"Whoever did it must've clubbed Wade down and left him in the backhouse," he said. "Then come in here and shot Cable."

"Cable got it from the front and with his gun out," Todd went on. "It'd take a real good man with a gun to face him and walk away at the end."

"We've got to let the boss know," Jeavons stated.

"Yeah," agreed Freeman without enthusiasm.

"And soon," Todd continued, making no attempt to leave.

Glancing at his two companions, Jeavons read mutiny on their faces. Although they both stood taller, neither could equal his speed with a gun and that fact gave him a moral ascendancy over them. If it came to a point, Jeavons figured that he now stood second to the boss; Cable's death putting him in that position. He had enough sense to know that forcing the issue would not improve his chances of bene-fiting from his advanced station in life.

"There's nothing we can do here," he said. "So we'll *all* go down to the saloon and see the boss."

While Freeman and Todd did not relish the idea of going out on the street again in the darkness, they cared to stay at the jail even less. That same unseen man who struck down and badly injured Bialowski and Tupper had now beaten Cable in what appeared to have been a fair fight. Doubtless he was still around, lurking in the darkness and just waiting for a chance to do further damage. If he decided to strike again, everything would be in his favor. Not that going on the street offered them a better chance, except that there the odds would be three to one instead two of them against the mysterious stranger.

"Let's go," Todd suggested.

"Keep out to the center of the street," Jeavons ordered. "And if anything moves, shoot first then start asking questions."

Each man cast a glance at the rear door, remembering the discarded shotguns lying beyond it. Much as they would like to have the heavy scatter-guns in their hands, not one of them wanted to chance opening the door and making the collection. Instead they went to the wall rack and helped themselves to a Winchester rifle each. Although the Winchester was less effective for their purpose than a shotgun, none of them mentioned the fact. After loading the rifles, they left the jail and walked along the street.

Fortunately everybody in town had taken the marshal's warning seriously and remained indoors, although eyes studied the trio of men from behind curtains in more than one house. If anybody had made an appearance, the trio would have followed Jeavon's advice without hesitation. Seeing nobody and hearing nothing to worry them, the three men arrived at the saloon without incident.

Jeavons knew better than walk unannounced into the saloon under the prevailing conditions. To do so courted sudden death, for the occupants of the room must have heard the shooting. So he halted in the street and called his name loudly.

"Come ahead!" replied Claibourne's voice.

Even after taking the precautions, Jeavons found two shotguns lined on him as he entered the barroom. Digby and Braun, normally employed as bouncers, stood in defensive positions behind the counter. Not until all three men entered the saloon did Claibourne make his appearance from behind the bar.

"What happened?" he asked as the trio approached the bar.

"Cable's dead," replied Jeavons. "And I want a drink."

"How did he die?" demanded the town boss.

"Down at the jail while we made the rounds. He was shot."

"Where's Wade?" yelped Claibourne, suddenly realizing that there should be four men present.

"He's dead, too," growled Jeavons, taking the drink which Digby poured out for him.

"But who—" began Claibourne.

"You tell me," Jeavons replied. "Jack Cable was pretty fast with a gun."

"So?"

"So he'd been shot in the front and in what looked like a fair fight."

"And you never saw the man who did it?"

"Nary sight nor sound, boss," said Jeavons.

While Claibourne would have preferred to hear the news in private, he knew it was too late for that. Glancing at his men, he read concern and a hint of fear on each face. So he struggled to prevent showing any of the anxiety which gnawed at him. With Cable and Wade dead, he could rely upon only the men present. Although recovered, Bialowski could only limp slowly and was of no use in a fight. Maybe Gosling and some more of the lesser lights of Claibourne's organization would side with their employer, but he preferred not to rely upon their help. No, if he hoped to retain his hold of the town, he must handle it with his remaining five men.

"We've got to get whoever it is that's doing it," Claibourne stated.

"Tonight," Jeavons asked. "In the dark?"

"That wouldn't be wise," admitted Claibourne.

To Jeavons's mind, it would be the height of folly. While the mysterious man could shoot, assured that he faced an enemy, Jeavons and his companions must ensure that they did not cut down on a friend. Dealing with a man fast enough to take Jack Cable in a fair fight, such a delay was certain to prove fatal.

"When do we do it, boss?" he asked.

"In the morning," replied Claibourne. "I've an idea that will bring him into the open and once he's there, we'll handle him."

While talking, Jeavons and Claibourne drew away from the others and the town boss nodded to where the quartet of hard-cases stood drinking and throwing nervous glances at the street doors.

"The men look jumpy."

"They are jumpy," Jeavons agreed. "It's the way this damned feller's acting. If he'd once come out in the open—"

"Which's why he doesn't," Claibourne explained. "He can handle us better the way he's doing it. This way he's making the men so they don't know whether they're dealing with a man or a ghost."

"I never went much on a haunt that handled folks like he done with Al and Stan. Nor one that could handle a .45 good enough to kill Jack Cable. It's a man, not a ghost we're after—but happen we get him in the open, he'll soon be a haunt."

"I've an idea how we can do it," the town boss stated. "Once he's dead, we can soon get this town back where we want it."

* * *

Daylight came and soon people started to appear on Gallup Creek's main street. Clearly they had only been restraining their curiosity through fear of Cable's gun-backed curfew and gathered in talking groups. Although many people showed an interest in the jail, Jeavons had men in front of it to prevent too close an inspection. Speculation ran rife, as he could plainly see and he detected a new air about the people. Unless something could be done quickly, Claibourne's hold on the town would be gone.

"All right, boys," Jeavons said, throwing a glance around him. "Let's go and get it done."

Although Dave Cleat stood sweeping the sidewalk before the Wells Fargo office, he paid little attention to the men who crossed the street. Going up the three steps on to the sidewalk, Digby and Todd approached the young man. Jeavons came to a halt with Braun still on the street and swung to face the small but growing knot of people on the opposite sidewalk. Before Dave Cleat could make a move, Digby and Todd caught him by the arms. The broom clattered to the sidewalk and the two men started to haul their captive towards the steps.

"All right, you bunch!" Jeavons called. "Somebody worked over Bialowski and Tupper, and killed Jack Cable. We don't know who did it, but unless we find out by noon we aim to hang this kid."

At which point Dave Cleat showed his objection to being used as a hostage. Digby, gripping Dave's right arm, descended the steps to the street and forced his captive to follow. Balancing himself on his left foot, Dave Cleat raised his right leg so that it passed over Digby's right arm then drove down between it and the left to smash with considerable force into the man's belly. So unexpectedly and with such force did the blow arrive that Digby gave a startled squawk and lost his hold. Clutching his middle and bent over to try to relieve the pain, Digby staggered backwards.

If Dave Cleat acted in wild panic, he scored a success. An attack on Todd might have produced an immediate release, but Digby, being lower than the captive, stood a better chance of throwing Dave off his balance.

Only the small man had not acted in a panic-inspired move but with deadly thought-out purpose. On being freed from Digby's grasp, Dave kept his right leg raised and pivoted around to the left. Out drove his right boot to collide savagely with Todd's groin. Agony knifed into the man, causing him to release Dave's other wrist and double over clutching at the injured area.

Even as Jeavons and Braun realized that things were going wrong, Dave shot out his left hand. Catching hold of Todd's vest, Dave gave a heave which hauled the man forward and propelled him off the sidewalk to crash into Digby. In passing, Dave's other hand slid Todd's revolver from its holster. Ignoring the sight of Digby and Todd crashing to the ground, Dave gave his attention to Jeavons.

Too late the hard-case saw his danger, finding that the small stranger held a Colt revolver. More than that, Dave Cleat handled the gun in a mighty proficient manner which sent a warning to Jeavons's brain. Suddenly, in a strange way, Dave Cleat stopped being a small, insignificant drifter; put on size and heft until he gave the impression of towering over every other man present.

Swiftly, far too swiftly for mere chance to guide his actions, Dave Cleat went into a crouched position. Knees slightly bent, legs apart and facing squarely at Jeavons, with spine slanted forward, right arm carried directly forward from the shoulder, right elbow about six inches ahead of the right hip-bone, with the forearm level as if to form an extension of the revolver's barrel, Dave Cleat adopted the style of shooting used by the top names of the gun-fighting fraternity—and did it with practiced, lightning fast ease. Flame lashed from the Colt's barrel and its bullet caught Jeavons in the chest before the man could shoot. Jeavons jerked under the impact, spun around and fell to the ground.

Even as he fired, Dave Cleat flung himself in a turning dive under the sidewalk's hitching rail. He missed death by inches as Braun's bullet fanned the air above him. Landing on the street, Dave fired and his bullet caught Braun in the ribs. Although hit, Braun did not drop his revolver and Dave shot again without hesitation. He acted as a trained lawman would under the circumstances, driving home a second bullet and being ready to continue shooting until the other man let the revolver fall and dropped himself. Again lead tore into Braun and his fingers opened, allowing the Colt to fall from them. Staggering, the man dropped to the street's surface.

Still reacting at the same speed which characterized his actions from the first movement on the sidewalk, Dave Cleat covered Digby and Todd. Having untangled themselves, they sat up and began to reach for weapons—although in Todd's case no revolver awaited his grabbing hand.

"Hold it!" Dave barked.

"Come on!" yelled the butcher and ran forward.

Given such a lead, the men of the town followed. They descended on the two hard-cases in a swarm. Hands grabbed hold of the two men and hauled them erect and a sea of angry faces surrounded them.

"Get a rope!" somebody yelled.

"That's enough!" barked the man called Dave Cleat and something in his voice brought silence to the crowd. "There'll be no lynching."

"We've stood plenty from this pair and all Claibourne's bunch!" one of the crowd pointed out.

"Likely," said the small Texan quietly. "They're only the hired men. Where at's their boss?"

For a moment the men had forgotten the chief cause of their misery. Once reminded of Claibourne, they put aside thoughts of lynching the two hard-cases. The butcher jerked his head towards the saloon.

"He'll likely be at the Rocking Horse. Say, are you Dusty Fog?"

"I've been called that at times," replied the small Texan. "Let's go and get Claibourne afore he can organize a defense."

The time Claibourne feared had come. At last the citizens of Gallup Creek found themselves with a leader, a man of courage and possessing the ability to form them into a fighting force. Angry rumbles rose from the crowd, voices raised in suggestions. Many of the assembled men carried revolvers concealed on their persons and others prepared to collect rifles or shotguns should such be needed.

"Dusty!" called a voice, and the Reverend Hocknell came around the corner.

"It's near on over, Tom," the small Texan replied. "We've only got to take Claibourne and it'll be done."

"Let the men from town do it," Hocknell suggested. "You've done enough."

"The Reverend's right, boys," shouted the butcher. "Cap'n Fog's fought our fight for long enough. Let's go."

Apart from a quartet of grimly determined men who stood guard over the prisoners and Doctor Smith working on the badly wounded Jeavons, almost the whole male population of Gallup Creek started along the street towards the saloon.

"It's for the best, Dusty," Hocknell stated. "Let them handle their own affairs now you've built up their courage, or they'll be dependent on somebody to do their fighting all the time."

Before the men could reach the saloon, its batwing doors flew open and Gosling burst through.

"Don't shoot!" he yelled. "Claibourne's in the office, emptying the—"

A gun roared from inside the saloon. Gosling screamed, his back arched in pain and he blundered off the sidewalk to land face down on the street. Instead of ingratiating himself with the people of the town, he found death as a payment for betraying his employer.

Lowering his smoking Colt, Claibourne looked around the room. If it came to a fight he could rely upon only two of the occupants. Although Tupper still lay in a bed upstairs, immobilized by his broken ribs, Bialowski could walk well enough to be on hand. Freeman, standing by the window, also received pay for his fighting services. The other occupants merely worked in the saloon and had no stake in their employer's outside activities.

Nobody made any comment on the shooting of Gosling. Most of them considered it might be unwise to take any stand on the subject at that moment. Fury showed on Claibourne's face, as it had when he burst from the office in time to bring a halt to Goslin's treachery.

"Out the back way!" he yelled. "We'll make a run for the livery barn, grab horses and get the hell out of here."

Studying the heavy carpetbag in their boss's left hand, Bialowski and Freeman crossed the room to join him. That bag contained the money looted from the town, a sum sufficient to retain their loyalty. Joining their boss, they went into the private office and Freeman opened the rear door. A bullet struck its jamb, threw splinters into Freeman's face and caused a rapid withdrawal.

"They're getting the place surrounded!" Freeman yelped unnecessarily.

Once aroused, the townsmen moved fast. Sufficient of

them carried weapons to make the surrounding of the saloon feasible and, under the butcher's urgings, men darted down the alley between the buildings so as to cover the rear. They came into sight in time to prevent the departure of Claibourne's party.

Standing at his office window, Claibourne watched men taking over at different places so they could sweep the rear of the saloon with fire. So far he could see only revolvers, but knew others of the crowd would be speeding to their homes where rifles and shotguns awaited them.

"What about it, boss?" Bialowski asked, conscious that his injured back prevented him from moving at any speed.

Before Claibourne could answer, the decision was taken clean out of his hands. At the office door stood the three male saloon employees who had been present and each of them held a weapon aimed at Claibourne's party.

"Wh—What's this?" gulped Claibourne, but he knew the answer.

"This's a nice lil town," the boss bartender replied, his Colt lined at Claibourne's belly. "I'm settled comfortable here and don't feel like moving."

"Which same folks'll feel less like moving us on happen we take you three out to 'em," stated the faro dealer, secure behind the comforting barrels of a ten gauge, sawed-off shotgun.

"Alive or dead won't make no never mind to how they feel about us," the grizzled old bouncer continued, handling his revolver with casual skill. "So let them guns drop peaceable like."

More than anything, the shotgun proved the decisive factor of the argument. At close range its cut-down barrels sprayed lead in a mighty effective manner and could likely include all three men in its pattern. Slowly Bialowski opened his hand to let his gun fall to the ground. Its thud appeared to jar Freeman into movement, although the hard-case did no more than follow Bialowski's lead.

"Now you, Mr. Claibourne!" said the dealer.

For a moment Claibourne hesitated, thoughts racing through his mind. In his left hand he felt the heavy weight of the carpetbag full of money. Inside the bag lay the results of his stay in Gallup Creek; sufficient wealth to keep him in comfort while searching for and taking over another small town. To surrender meant standing trail—always assuming that the citizens allowed the affair to reach a courtroom. Somehow he believed that they would; if only because Dusty Fog had never been the kind of man to permit lynch law. Claibourne had legal training and knew just how difficult it would be to prove him guilty of properly constituted court. At no time had he taken part in the performance of an illegal act and proving that he planned or organized the actions of his men would be so difficult that a skilled lawyer might easily prevent it.

Then Claibourne remembered Gosling. Up until killing the man, he might have slipped through the meshes of the law's net. That one act changed everything. Too many people with too much to lose had seen him fire the fatal shot for him to worm out of the consequences of his act. Fury boiled up inside Claibourne; the same type of blind rage which caused him to shoot Gosling in punishment for his attempted betrayal.

"Damn you!" he screeched and started to lift his revolver.

Instantly Bialowski and Freeman flung themselves away from their employer's sides. Possibly a real top hand with a gun might have been able to move fast enough to do something, but Claibourne lacked the necessary speed. The faro dealer's right forefinger depressed the shotgun's trigger and its twelve inch barrels kicked high under the recoil caused by exploding black powder throwing a load of buckshot out of the right tube. Four .32 caliber balls caught Claibourne in the chest, slamming back into the wall. His gun slipped from limp fingers and clattered to the floor and the carpetbag dropped with a solid thud at the other side. Then Claibourne's feet slid outwards and his body sank down until he sat on the floor, but he was dead.

Curses left Bialowski at the pain caused to his sore spine by crashing heavily down. Glancing around, he found a revolver lined on him and made no attempt to move. Also lying on the floor, Freeman spread his arms over his head to ensure that the old swamper knew he had no intention of sharing their late employer's folly.

"Best go tell the folks to come in and take over," suggested the dealer. "I reckon they'll be pleased to get their town back."

"I think you might have told me who you were, Dusty," Mary Hocknell said in an agrieved tone which brought chuckles from the men seated around the dining room table of her home.

It was the night of the big clean-up day and the Reverend Hocknell gave a dinner for a few friends in celebration. Although Dusty Fog no longer wore the cast-off clothing, he still looked much the same insignificant cowhand.

"Your pappy and I decided it would be better if you didn't know," he explained. "Not because we didn't trust you, but because we figured you'd be safer not knowing."

"How did you come to be here, Captain Fog?" asked Doctor Smith. "We thought that Claibourne had the mail bottled up."

"Maybe he could've stopped a letter going to the Rangers, or anywhere that he knew would be to somebody who'd stop his game," Dusty answered. "But he didn't check everything that left town. Tom wrote to a friend, told him what was happening here and asked him to send for the Rangers. Instead, the friend sent word to Uncle Devil and he told me to come over and see what was doing."

"But why did you come in looking like a saddletramp?" the butcher inquired. "I'd've expected you to bring the rest of the floating outfit with you."

"They were all away from the spread handling different chores," Dusty replied. "So I came up alone, figured to learn how things stood and if I need to wait for the rest of the boys to join me. Only I met Wally Harris on the trail and he told me how things stood. When I heard how few men Claibourne hired, I figured that I might be able to stir the folks in town up, get them to handle things."

"You sure had everybody fooled," grinned the doctor. "Those clothes and that horse—"

"I took Wally over to Sam Dexter's ranch, Sam being an old friend. Fact being that Sam didn't like the way things were going in town, but had all his best men off handling a trail herd. That's why I decided to play things the way I did. I reckon to let folks know I was around ready to back them, but not ready to show my hand until I'd learned who I could trust and what my chances were of getting help."

"Did you send that deputy's body in across his saddle?" the butcher wanted to know. "Bialowski told us that you did, but we never saw it."

"I'd had to shoot the deputy to save Wally Harris," Dusty told him. "So I figured to hand Claibourne's bunch a shock. I let the hoss loose hoping it would come down the main drag where folks would see it, but it went around to the livery barn and that Gosling jasper went straight to Claibourne. They buried the deputy without folks knowing what had happened."

"Rollinson from the bank saw the horse come in, but didn't go near it," the doctor remarked. "Word had got around, although we didn't know who killed the deputy until you left the note after working Bialowski and Tupper over. Say, did you go after them because of what they did to you when you came into town?"

"Nope," admitted Dusty. "Although finding it was them didn't make me feel unhappy. I'd slipped out of the house here looking for a chance to stir Claibourne and his crew up. I figured if I showed that they could be licked, the folks in town would be ready to fight back."

"But how did a feller your si—" began the butcher, his words wavering off as he wondered how Dusty might take any reference to his lack of inches. "How'd you manage to handle them two?"

"Surprise helped. And Uncle Devil has a Japanese servant, fellow who come back here with Commodore Perry. Tommy Okasi knows some mighty fancy fighting tricks and he taught me most of them. He calls the way he fights jujitsu and karate and you can believe me that they give me a real edge in a fight."

"Don't let Dusty's size fool you, Fred," Hocknell warned the butcher. "I'd match him against any man in town for strength. I tell you, Dusty, I nearly gave the whole game away when I felt your biceps under that ragged shirt when we first met. Then I realized that a feller as strong as you must have a reason for not fighting back."

"Reckon I owe you more than most folks in town, Captain," the butcher stated. "I was set to face Cable this morning, rather than pay any more. I couldn't've done it and lived."

"That's why I saw him last night," Dusty replied. "I'd been watching you folks and reckon you'd be ready to stand up for yourself. So I went to even the odds."

"You had your guns in the warbag when you arrived," the doctor said, but Dusty shook his head.

"No. That held nothing more than a drifter would carry. I'd hidden my clothes, gunbelt and guns outside town and collected them after dark the first night."

"You sure had everybody fooled, though," enthused the butcher. "When we heard that Dusty Fog was backing us, we knew we could face up to Claibourne, but nobody even started to think that you—"

A smile came to Dusty's face as once more the butcher brought excited words to a halt. It had been many years since he last worried about people failing to recognize him. Of course most folks could not reconcile the small, insignificant cowhand with the legendary Dusty Fog. That fact had been useful before and Dusty did not doubt but that it would come in handy again.

"I've always heard that you—" the doctor started to say.

"Stand over six foot tall," Dusty finished for him. "I've heard that too. It's a natural enough mistake. Most folks take Mark Counter for me."

PART TWO

The Death of Henry Urko

Without a doubt Mark Counter looked how popular conception imagined Dusty Fog should be. Six foot three inches tall, with an almost classically handsome face and golden blond hair, wide shoulders which tapered down to a slender waist, possessed of a giant's muscular development, he looked like a god of old; or just how a traditional hero ought to be.

Not that Mark stopped off with only looks. He could claim to be a tophand and, if anything, more capable in matters pertaining to the cattle handling business than his good friend, Dusty Fog. Although so well-developed, he moved fast and light on his feet; a fact which would have been profanely attested to by anybody who ran against him during a roughhouse brawl. Although folks often spoke of Mark's prowess in the bare-handed fighting line, they rarely mentioned his ability with a gun. Yet the few who knew gave him credit for being second only to Dusty in the matter of speedy withdrawal and accurate use of his two matched, ivory handled Colt Cavalry Peacemakers.

Always a dandy dresser, Mark looked even more so while

strolling along Trail Street, Mulrooney, the latest of a series of Kansas trail-end towns. After receiving his pay at the end of a trail drive, any cowhand could be expected to fancy himself up a mite. However few of them ever looked really at home or comfortable in their town-bought clothes. Mark wore a Texas style white Stetson with a silver concha decorated band around it, grey cutaway jacket made to his fit by a tailor who could claim to be a better craftsman than found in most Western towns, frilly-bosomed white shirt, string tie, fancy vest, tight legged white trousers and town boots which bore a shine to reflect the scenery; and looked completely at ease in them.

Born the third son of a Texas rancher who owned a spread only slightly smaller than the OD Connected, wealthy in his own right due to a maiden aunt leaving him all her considerable fortune when she died, Mark might have lived a life of leisure or owned his own place. Instead he preferred to ride as a working cowhand, acting as Dusty Fog's able right bower in time of trouble and serving as a leading member of the floating outfit. During the Civil War, as a lieutenant in Bushrod Sheldon's cavalry, Mark's ideas of military uniform set the fashion for the other young Southern bloods. Currently his sartorial tastes dictated what the well-dressed Texas cowhand wore. However once in a while he liked to wear something different to range clothes and grabbed at any excuse which gave him the chance to do so.

When an invitation reached Dusty Fog requesting attendance at a formal dinner given by the Mulrooney Businessmen's Association, it aroused little enthusiasm or desire to accept among the members of the floating outfit. In fact all but Mark promptly produced almost valid reasons why they should be excused. So Mark found himself elected to represent the OD Connected, on the grounds that he alone of the floating outfit possessed the necessary fancy do-dads in which to attend the dinner.

Although Mark would have preferred to spend the night in the less formal, but more entertaining, society to be found at Freddie Woods' Fair Lady Saloon, he went to the dinner. All in all it had not been too bad, neither more nor less boring than he expected and with excellent food. At its end he made his excuses, avoiding invitations to play poker or go on a spree with some of the other diners and set off to rejoin his friends.

During the day and early evening, the section of Trail Street along which Mark walked would have been very busy. At that hour of the night, the stores were closed and the hotel which stood amongst them looked deserted. Further along the street could be heard the sound of cowhand revelry, rising from the saloons, dancehalls, gambling houses and theater which occupied that section. Mark directed his feet in that direction, knowing he would find his friends there. As he approached the alley separating the hotel from a leather-ware shop, Mark heard voices.

"It's her all right, Stash," said one.

"Looks that way, Waldo," growled a deep voice, also male. "Where's he—"

"Get your hands off me!" a woman cried, her voice holding a hint of panic.

Cautiously Mark stepped forward and looked into the alley. Overhead a full moon threw out enough light for him to see everything. A trio of men wearing town style clothing surrounded a very pretty, shapely young woman. At her right, the big, bulky jasper with a heavy walrus moustache carried on speaking:

"Don't be loco, Silvie. We've got you now and we aim to have you tell us."

"You'd best talk, sister," the skinny beanpole at the girl's left went on. "Old Stash's mean when he gets riled."

"And me 'n old Skinny here's the same," stated the man with his back to Mark, a flashy-dresser who came between the other two in build. "Let's get her away from here so we can talk."

A prudent man might have walked on in the hope of meeting one of the city's deputy marshals; a suspicious man could even have suspected a trap laid to lure an unwary gallant down the alley to be beaten over the head and robbed. Prudence had never been Mark's prime virtue. While not entirely unaware of the second contingency, Mark ignored it. If the girl aimed to act as a decoy, she ought to be making more noise to ensure he heard her. More than that, although he could see little of her, she did not strike him as the usual type to become involved with that kind of game. With that point in mind, Mark turned into the alley's mouth and moved forward. If the girl needed help, he figured to give it to her. Should it be a trap, well he reckoned he could supply the answer to that despite having left his gunbelt and Colts at the Fair Lady.

Moving silently, Mark closed the gap with the group and the girl first became aware of his presence. A look of amazement, mingled with shock came to her tense face and her mouth dropped open. However she did not cry out, but struggled harder so as to hold the attention of the three men.

"Damn you, gal!" Stash snarled as her foot hacked his shin. "I'll—"

At which point Skinny became the first member of the trio to notice the advancing blond giant. In a way the thin man almost mirrored the girl's reaction on seeing Mark and his behavior attracted his companions' attention. Releasing the girl, Stash started to swing around in Mark's direction.

Mark lunged forward, his hands clamping hold of Waldo

by the shoulders and hoisting the man into the air. Even before Waldo could feel shocked to find himself lifted in such a casual manner, Mark hurled him at Stash. The two collided, staggering backwards. In a continuation of the move, Mark's right arm swung across in a back-hand slap which spun Skinny around like a child's top and sent him into the wall. Thrusting Waldo aside, Stash charged at Mark in a wild rush. Avoiding the man, Mark drove his fist against the other's ear. Stash yelped, shot off his original course and sprawled face down to plough along the ground with his chin.

"Look out!" the girl yelled.

Even though she gave him nothing more to go on, Mark knew that danger could only come from one source. Turning, he found his assumption to be correct. Waldo came forward, his hand emerging from a jacket pocket with something metallic glinting on the knuckles. Lunging forward, Waldo threw a blow aimed to drive his fist and its deadly brass sheath into Mark's face. If the brass knuckles landed, they packed enough power to tear open flesh and inflict sufficient pain to make the recipient all but helpless. Only to do so they had to land. Up shot Mark's hand to catch Waldo's out-driving wrist. A screech broke from Waldo as he felt a terrible pressure which seemed to be crushing his very bones. Savagely Mark chopped his other fist into Waldo's belly. Then he crashed the trapped hand against the wall. Pain made Waldo open his fingers and Mark dragged the hand along the wall and tore off the brass knuckles.

Before Mark could finish Waldo, Skinny took a hand once more. Running forward, the lean man leapt on to Mark's back, locking legs about his body, throwing one arm about his throat while the other hand reached around to feel for his eyes. Stash was also up and attacking. His right fist drove into Mark's belly, then the left slammed into the blond giant's jaw. Twisting his head in an effort to avoid Skinny's fingers, Mark brought up his foot. As Stash swung another punch, Mark placed the sole of his foot against the man's body and thrust. The force of the shove sent Stash hurling away to collide with the wall.

Skinny's bony fingers found Mark's eyes and the blond giant jerked his head just in time. Removing the man from his back became of the most vital importance and Mark figured he knew just how to do it. Throwing himself backwards, Mark carried Skinny across the alley and crashed him into the wall. Powered by Mark's great muscles, the full force of his two hundred pound body crushed Skinny against the unyielding timbers of the leather-ware shop. Skinny gave a croaking gasp, his arms and legs lost their grips and he collapsed to the ground.

Showing more courage than sense, Waldo rushed into the attack. It may have been that he thought Mark to be off balance. If so, he soon learned differently. Freed from Skinny's weight. Mark could move at his usual speed; a factor which Waldo failed to take into consideration when starting his charge. Seeing the danger, in the shape of Mark's bunched fist driving straight at him, Waldo tried to come to a stop. He failed and ran full into the punch, adding his forward impetus to its power. Caught by the fist, Waldo appeared to be trying to go two ways at once. While his legs continued their forward movement, his upper torso went the opposite direction until his feet left the ground and he crashed down on to his back.

While Mark dealt with Skinny and Waldo, Stash came into the attack. In rushing forward he had to pass the girl and she took her first active part in the proceedings. Drawing up the hem of her skirt, she thrust a shapely foot between Stash's legs and tripped him. Mark swung around from felling Waldo, side-stepped the off-balance Stash, driving a boot into his rump as he passed. Already unable to stop himself, Stash increased speed under the impulse of Mark's kick and went head first into the wall. Bouncing back, Stash landed in a rag-doll limp manner which told anyone wise in such matters that he would not be rising again.

Turning, Mark looked at the girl and grinned. Then he saw her sway, hand going to her throat, and he sprang to her side.

"Are you all right, ma'am?" he asked, slipping an arm around her waist to steady her.

"I—I—Could you take me from here, please?"

"Into the hotel?"

"N—No. To the railroad depot."

"I reckon I can do that," admitted Mark and nodded to the three men. "How about them?"

"They aren't d—dead?" gasped the girl.

"Nope. I figured you might want them tossing into the hoosegow—"

"The hoosegow?" she repeated, sounding puzzled.

"Jail. What were they after you for?"

"I've no idea," she replied. "To rob me, perhaps."

"Then I should get the marshal—" Mark began.

"Oh, no. Please!" the girl gasped. "If you do there will be questions and I may miss the night train to Newton. Can't we just leave them here and forget it?"

"I reckon so," Mark drawled. "I'll see you to the train."

While Mark would willingly agree to escort a real pretty young woman, more than his normal Southern gallantry lay behind his decision. Every instinct he possessed told him that there was more to the affair than met the eye. While escorting the girl from the alley, he studied her. She wore good quality clothing, stylish and in perfect taste. Although her voice seemed well-bred, he could not place its accent. Nor did her behavior fit in with her general appearance.

Why had she not started screeching at the top of her voice for help when the three jaspers jumped her as one might expect? Mark would have thought that to be a girl of her type's first reaction. Nor did the conversation he overheard before taking a hand lead him to believe the trio were strangers. Learning the answers to the puzzling aspects might prove interesting.

"Nobody saw or heard the fight," the girl said as she and Mark walked along the street.

"Looks that way," he answered. "Can't say I'm sorry. I'm not looking to meet the local law if I can help it."

"Oh—" said the girl, flashing an interested and appraising glance his way. "Why is that?"

"Let's say we see things a different way."

Mark could not imagine why he made the two statements. However they achieved a result in making the girl look even harder at him. She studied his clothes and lifted her eyes once more to his face. It appeared that she did not object to being in the company of a man with an aversion to meeting peace officers.

"Do you work here?" she asked.

"Nope."

"Why not?"

"Let's say that I don't like the way things are run here."

This time Mark spoke with a definite purpose. During the early days of Mulrooney he served as a deputy marshal in town and watched Dusty Fog frame the laws which made it unique among the Kansas trail-ends. Crooked gamblers and other petty criminals found the going hard in Mulrooney, being actively discouraged by the current town marshal in carrying out the work Dusty started. If the girl knew anything about Mulrooney, she ought to form the conclusion he wanted.

"You haven't anything to hold you in town?" she said,

sounding just a mite too casual.

"I reckon not."

"Then will you help me? I do so need help."

"I've never yet refused to help a pretty lady," Mark assured her.

"Perhaps I had best tell you the truth then," she said, dropping her voice to a confiding whisper. "I lied when I said I didn't know those three men."

"Likely you had your reasons," Mark replied, trying to sound surprised.

"Yes, I have. They were hired to prevent my brother and I reaching the Canadian border by the end of the month?"

"Now why'd they want to do a mean thing like that?" asked Mark.

"Because if we don't get there, we will lose a fortune left by our uncle in his will."

"You will, huh?" Mark said, with the kind of interest the girl expect appeared to expect. "How'd that be?"

"You see our uncle, he was our only surviving relative, made a fortune trading in Canada. He always kept us in luxury and I'm afraid that we neglected him. You know how it is, we were always too busy with our social life to bother about writing and thanking him, or things like that. Well, it hurt Uncle Randle and he made his will in such a manner that we have to do something or lose it."

"So that's why you're out here."

"Yes," agreed the girl. "Henry and I have had to collect various items, letters and the like that Uncle Randle sent to various friends. While I came here to pick up a letter, Henry had to go to a small village and will meet me in Newton."

"And those three jaspers aim to stop you getting there," Mark commented.

"They do. You see, Uncle Randle added a clause that if Henry and I don't arrive at Bannock in the proscribed time, the entire fortune goes to his partner."

"You shouldn't have any more trouble with those three, that's for sure," Mark drawled, watching the girl from the corner of his eye.

While he had considerable experience in the matter of reading facial expression, being a good poker player, he failed to detect anything in the girl's attitude. There did seem to be a slight hesitation in her answering his comments, but that might mean only a marshalling of facts so as to explain the more fully.

"There's enough at stake for the partner to have more men at work," she told him after another of the brief pauses. "That's why I would like you to escort me to Newton. Of course I'm willing to reimburse any expenses for you."

"I'd do it for free," Mark drawled. "But if you insist I might let you stand me a meal at the Cattlemen's Hotel in Newton."

Happen the girl told the truth, she needed help and Mark was only too willing to supply it. If she should be lying for some reason, learning why might prove both interesting and entertaining. At the worst he could enjoy the girl's company as far as Newton and then return to Mulrooney. Dusty did not intend to head back to Texas for a few days and Mark could easily make the trip to Newton and back in time to accompany his friends on the ride home. Even if he failed to see anybody at the depot who might take word to his friends, the remainder of the floating outfit were unlikely to worry about his disappearance. Most likely they would attribute it to the correct cause, that he went off some place in the company of a right pretty young lady.

"As we'll be traveling together, we may as well introduce ourselves," the girl remarked, breaking in on his thoughts. "My name is Silvia Urko, but most of my friends call me Silvie."

"Then I surely hope you count me as a friend, Silvie," Mark drawled. "My name's Matson, Mark Matson."

Either the girl did not know his true identity, or she accepted his alias without question. Whichever way, she made no comment and they approached the depot where the train stood waiting to depart. Mark began to feel puzzled, wondering how the girl came to be traveling with no more baggage than the vanity bag which hung from her left wrist.

Like most trains which ran the Western tracks, the one waiting at the depot carried both passengers and freight. Not unexpectedly, Silvie headed for the Pullman car which offered more comfortable accommodation than that of the day cars on the other side of the diner. Standing at the platform entrance to the car, the conductor held out his hand for the tickets.

"We'll have to get them on the train," Mark told him, glancing around.

Much to his relief, Mark saw nobody he recognized and who might inadvertently let slip his true identity. The conductor did not know him and the depot staff were fully occupied elsewhere. Only a small crowd gathered and they all appeared to be involved in saying their good-byes to passengers.

"Sure," the conductor replied. "Get aboard."

"Henry!" Silvie suddenly gasped. "The baggage! It's by the depot there."

"I'll have a grip fetch it for you, ma'am," sniffed the conductor and muttered something under his breath, the only part of which Mark caught was a reference to "damned blow-ins"; the railroader's name for passengers who arrived just as the train prepared to pull out.

"They're the four brown leather bags," Silvie began unnecessarily, for only four bags now stood by the depot door.

"And do ask your man to be more careful than the other. He scratched them badly."

"I'll tell him to take real special care, ma'am," promised the conductor impatiently. "If you'll both get aboard—"

Taking Silvie's arm, Mark assisted her into the car and they found seats with no trouble due to a lack of passengers. Mark scanned the length of the train, watching through the window for any sign of the trio who caused fuss for the girl. The arrival of the "grip", porter, with the bags coincided with the first movement of the train. After tipping the man, Mark resumed his watch. Slowly, but gathering speed, the train drew away from the depot and by the stockyards. At last Mark sat back in his seat and relaxed.

"Those three *hombres* aren't aboard," he told Silvie. "Or if they are, they must have slipped on from the other side."

"Do you think they might have?" the girl asked.

"Nope," Mark replied, then looked down at the bags. "Say they have been scratched up."

Although the bags were well-made, expensive pieces, with their owner's name marked on them, bad scratches all but removed the lettering. With an effort Mark managed to read "H. Urko" on each one.

"Henry will be furious when he sees them," Silvie answered. "Naturally I reported the man who did it, but that hasn't repaired the damage."

"How'd he manage to do it?" Mark inquired.

"I—I'm not sure," the girl replied. "Tell me something about yourself. We know so little about each other and I've made a start by telling you about me."

Clearly the girl did not want too close a discussion into the damage to her baggage, so Mark launched into a fictitious account of his life and left her with the impression that he spent his time hovering on the fringe of the law. As she showed no concern at his habits. Mark knew that she must have some ulterior motive for wanting him along as her escort. When he tried to learn more about the girl, she repeated the story of her uncle's will and then yawned and claimed that she felt tired.

For a comparatively short run like the one from Mulrooney to Newton, the Pullman crew did not bother to set up the sleeping bunks. However the upholstery of the seats was comfortable and Silvie nestled her head on Mark's shoulder with a contented sigh. To all intents she went to sleep and Mark relaxed. Obviously he would learn no more for a time and so he let the matter rest.

"Yes, my brother and I will take breakfast."

On hearing the words Mark stirred, opened his eyes and looked around. Clearly he had slept through the night for daylight streamed in at the car's windows. At his side, the girl looked up at the white-uniformed dining car attendant.

"Good morning, He—Mark," she went on, turning a smiling face to the blond giant. "Did you sleep well?"

"Well enough," Mark replied. "Where are we?"

"Soon be in Newton, sir," the Negro attendant replied. "But the train'll be there long enough for you-all to eat breakfast and still get off."

"Let's go eat it then," Mark drawled.

As the attendant said, the train arrived while they ate, but it had to take on freight before leaving. So Silvie and Mark finished a good meal without hurrying and on leaving the dining car found a porter waiting.

"Is you-all Mr. Urko, sir?" the man asked, indicating the bags.

"They're mine," Mark replied. "But my name's Matson."

"Ah understands, sah."

Something in the man's tone attracted Mark's attention. Clearly the man thought that the damage had been done deliberately and with the intention of obliterating the owner's name. An idea began to form in Mark's head, supplying the answer to some of the things puzzling him about the girl. Before it could take full shape something happened to remove it momentarily from his mind.

Along the track, not far from where he and the girl stood, a crew of lumpers* hauled a large traction engine slowly up a twin rail metal ramp into the freight car.

"That dinger's asking for trouble," growled the train's conductor who waited by the dining car, nodding to where a yardmaster stood between the tracks of the ramp so as to make sure all went smoothly.

"Sure is," Mark replied. "If one of those hauling ropes busts—"

Even as Mark spoke, something went wrong; although it was not the thing he suggested. Inside the freight car, the lumpers dragged in on the rope hand over hand, their combined strength slowly but surely hauling the engine up the ramp. Then one of the men at the rear slipped. Although he only lost his footing for a moment, the alteration in tension and weight distribution threw the entire team's effort out of focus.

Seeing the engine come to an abrupt halt and jolt back slightly, the yard-master took a hurried step to the rear. In doing so his foot caught against the next track's nearer rail and he sat down hard still between the bars of the ramp. A yell of fear burst from his lips as the engine slowly moved downwards. In the car, the lumpers fought to hold the weight and failed. All they could do was slow its downwards glide and its bulk prevented them from seeing the dinger sat full in the path of the engine.

Mark dragged himself free from Silvie's grasp as the girl

*Lumpers. Freightyard workers.

gasped and turned away from the sight. Springing forward, he halted spraddle-legged astride the terrified dinger and his hands raised to slap against the frame of the engine. Exerting all his strength, Mark fought to halt the downwards roll of the heavy mass of iron. At first it seemed that he must fail, for the engine's wheels continued to turn and it moved slowly onwards. With feet churning up the hard earth, arms bending a little and every muscle in his powerful body straining to its utmost, Mark felt the engine's weight forcing him back. Desperately he called on every reserve of strength he could muster and the movement downwards halted.

A low gasp broke from Silvie's lips and a concerted exclamation of amazement rolled through the crowd which had gathered. Never had they witnessed such a feat of strength and the sight halted them instead of goading them into assisting the blond giant. Even the lumpers in the train refrained from hauling on the ropes and the stopping of the engine fell entirely upon Mark's broad shoulders.

The conductor recovered first. Realizing that something must be done to help Mark, he acted with speed.

"Start hauling on the ropes, you lumpers!" he shouted. "Come on, some of you. Lend this gent a hand."

Given direction, the lumpers began to pull on the ropes once more and men from the crowd sprang forward. Eager hands laid hold of and pressed against the engine, assisting the efforts of the lumpers. Not until sure that the others had everything under control did Mark relax his pressure. Slowly the engine began to climb the ramp once more and Mark moved away. He stood with his head hanging, sweat soaking his face and shirt, fighting to regain his breath.

"Mark!" Silvie whispered, laying a hand on his arm. "Are you all right?"

"I reckon so," Mark replied after sucking in several deep breaths.

"Let's get away from here then. Please. We've thrown the men off our trail, so let's try to keep it that way."

"Sure," agreed Mark.

Slipping away unnoticed proved easier than either of them anticipated. The crowd gave its full attention to the engine as it slowly mounted the ramp once more under the combined efforts of the lumpers in the car and the men shoving from behind. Possibly most of the people watching hoped that they might see some further dramatic development, in which case they were to be disappointed. When the engine entered the car, its audience turned to praise the man who averted a tragedy and found that he had gone.

Although Silvie had shown a lack of knowledge about Western ways and affairs while talking with Mark, she clearly knew her way around Newton. Steering clear of the main part of town, she led Mark to a small, but comfortable-looking hotel in the better residential area.

"This's not the kind of place I usually stay in," Mark told her with truth.

"It's ideal for our purposes though," Silvie answered.

"I reckon I ought to have a shave and tidy up before we go in," Mark went on rubbing a hand across his jaw.

"It might be as well," she smiled. "I'll book the rooms while you go and we'll meet in the lounge when you're through."

The arrangement satisfied Mark and he left the girl at the hotel's entrance. Walking through the town he came to a barber's shop much patronized by Texas cowhands on being paid off from their trail herds. In addition to the usual services, the shop offered hot baths and the facilities of a tailor. While soaking in a hot bath, followed by a shave at the hands of the barber, Mark had his clothes tidied and pressed.

Never one to rush such a process, Mark spent something

over an hour at the barber's shop. Then he emerged, clean-shaven, bathed and dressed as immaculately as ever, although the shirt he bought to replace the one worn the previous evening did not fit quite so well as its predecessor, and made his way back to the hotel.

"Are you Mr. Matson?" asked the clerk behind the desk as Mark approached it.

"That's me."

"A young lady asked me to give you this letter when you came."

Mark took the bulky envelope from the man and hefted it in his hand. "Is she still here?"

"No. She came in, said you'd be along and left the letter is all."

"Thanks," Mark drawled and dropped a dollar on the desk.

Just as he turned, Silvie entered the hotel. A look of relief came to her face as she glanced at the unopened envelope and she crossed to his side.

"Mark. Thank heavens I found you," she gasped.

"What's up?" he asked.

"I saw those men, the ones we—met in Mulrooney. They're here in town."

"Let's go talk about it someplace a mite more private," Mark suggested, noting the interest on the clerk's face. "Say, this letter—"

"It was to tell you that I'd gone out for a short time," Silvie answered, taking the envelope from his hand, opening her vanity bag and dropping the bulky message into it.

Although the girl moved fast, Mark managed to look into the open mouth of the bag. Only one item attracted his interest, a Remington Double Derringer lying prominently fixed in a clip which held it readily accessible to a reaching hand. That clip had not been a recent attachment, which meant she should have been carrying the gun when the three men jumped her. Mark wondered why she did not use it. Another detail which Mark found interesting was why she needed such a bulky collection of paper to send him a short message, the envelope having been both thick and heavy.

"What do you aim to do about them?" he asked, putting aside the questions.

"I thought we might take the buggy I have waiting and leave town."

"Where're we going?"

"We could go north. Follow the spur line to the next town and then take a train to Brannock."

"That'll mean being on the trail at least until noon tomorrow," Mark warned.

"So?" Silvie asked.

"We'll be out there together all night."

"Will *that* bother you?" she smiled.

"Not if it doesn't bother you," Mark assured her. "You've your good name to think about."

"Why?" Silvie said, smiling in an inviting manner. "We're supposed to be brother and sister, aren't we?"

"Sure, but—"

"If it doesn't worry me, why should it bother you?"

"Put that way," Mark drawled. "It doesn't bother me at all. Let's go."

The pleasant prospect of spending the night alone with Silvie did not materialize. Taking Mark to the rear of town, Silvie showed him a two-horse buggy into which they climbed. While Mark took up the reins and drove, Silvie erected a parasol, rested it on her shoulder and sat close to him. Every instinct he possessed told Mark that he would soon learn what lay behind the girl's actions. However she made no mention of the subject and Mark felt inclined to wait until night before he pressed it.

After an hour of fast travel, the girl looked along their back trail and gave a sigh of relief.

"They're not following us. Let's rest the team, they've a long drive ahead."

"We'd best pull off the trail then," Mark answered.

"Why not go along this track?" Silvie suggested.

On taking the girl's advice, Mark found himself in a clearing out of sight of the trail and on the edge of a wide gorge. He halted the team and climbed down while the girl sat looking around her with interest.

"This looks just like a place where we used to picnic back East when I was a little girl," she declared. "Oh Mark, I must look around."

"Sure," Mark agreed indulgently and helped her to the ground. "Only don't go too close to the edge."

Despite Mark's warning and the ominous sounds from below, the girl walked to the edge of the gorge. Following her, Mark found exactly what he expected. Some fifty foot below a river tore its way between the walls, racing along and churning up white foam where it met a rock rising immovable from the bed. Further along the gorge, the river passed over a ledge to form a waterfall.

"I—I'm frightened!" Silvie gasped, moving hurriedly backwards and dropped her parasol in going.

"It's sure a wild water," Mark agreed, turning to join her.

"Oh Mark!" she said. "I dropped my parasol. Will you get it, please?"

Years of riding dangerous trails had given Mark an instinct for peril which sent a warning as he halted at the edge of the gorge. Bending to pick up the parasol, he glanced at the girl. She stood facing him, face expressionless as she drew the Derringer from her vanity bag. Straightening up, Mark saw her bring the wicked little gun shoulder high and take careful aim. Pure involuntary reaction made him forget his danger and take a pace back. Too late he realized where he stood and teetered on the very brink of the gorge. Then his foot slipped. He saw flame lick from the Derringer's upper barrel and next moment went pitching backwards, down towards the swirling water below.

Still holding her Remington and cocking it with practiced ease, Silvie walked to the edge of the gorge and looked down. She could see no sign of the blond giant, which did not entirely surprise her. Anybody who fell into that racing current would be swept downstream, probably under water, and carried over the fall.

"Poor Mark," she sighed, slipping the Remington back into her bag. "What a waste too. Still, it had to be done."

With that she returned to the buggy, climbed in, took up its reins and turned the horses, then drove away.

Although the bullet missed him by a couple of inches, Mark could not prevent himself going over the edge. Desperately he twisted himself over into a diving position as the water rushed closer. Expecting himself to crash on to jagged submerged rocks, he struck the surface of the river. Down he went, deeper and deeper, without feeling the impact or lacerations he expected and when his hands came into contact with the expected rocks, they proved to be the bottom of the river. Feeling the tug of the current, Mark struck out for the surface once more.

Luck had been with the blond giant, for the place he fell into proved to be a deep hole where the water eddied around in a slow swirl just off the main rush of the current. When his head broke surface, he appeared too close to the cliff for Silvie to be able to catch sight of him. By treading water, Mark found himself able to stay in the eddy until he regained his breath.

Before Mark could do more than fill his lungs, he found himself borne to the edge of the current again. Much as he wished he could devote time to thinking over the girl's motives he knew that he must first think about saving his life.

One quick-taken look warned Mark that he faced a difficult if not impossible task. Climbing the side of the gorge would be impossible at that point, or anywhere near, its walls being too steep and devoid of foot-holes. Nor did swimming downstream offer any greater prospect of success, for the current ran at an ever increasing pace until boiling over the waterfall. While there might be a deep hole under the falls in which he could land safely, Mark felt disinclined to chance it. Which only left going upstream— not much better than the other choices. As far as Mark could see from water level, the river ran fast and through the same kind of high walls.

However a small hope licked the be-jeesus out of no chance at all and Mark did not intend to go under without making one hell of a fight for life. Yet he did not rush into the business. First he peeled off his tie and slipped from the jacket allowing them both to float away followed by his vest. After quick thought he retained his boots. While they weighed heavily, or would later, he needed them should he survive the river to protect his feet during the five mile walk back to Newton.

Free of all excess weight, Mark thrust himself out of the deep eddy. Instantly he felt the drag of the racing current and struck out against it. Never had his great strength and superb physical fitness been put to such a test as he battled against the force of the river. Driving first one arm then the other forward, he dragged his giant frame through the water, his powerful legs kicking with all their strength. Almost by inches he advanced, knowing that the slightest pause would see him swept back the precious distance he gained.

Time ceased to have any meaning for Mark. He could not tell whether he had been fighting the river for seconds, minutes or hours. All he knew was that he must keep swimming. If he failed, Silvie's plan, whatever it might be, would work as well as if her bullet found its mark in him. Once he rested, allowing the current to hold him pressed against the upstream face of a rock which rose above the surface, until a growing chill warned him that he must move again. On two occasions he found easier water, deep eddies like the one in which he landed, and there floated until gathering strength for yet another effort. Then he went on again, fighting as he had before.

How long it was Mark had no way of knowing, but suddenly he became aware of a change. No longer did the gorge's walls rise sheer. Instead they slanted up in a slope which might be steep but could be climbed. The only problem remaining was to get ashore. Slowly Mark turned his aching body and struck out for the wide gravel spit which marked the edge of the water. Those last feet imposed a greater strain than Mark could ever remember. It seemed that he hung motionless in the current, unable to get any closer to the bank. Only by exercising all his will-power did he manage to keep swimming. Then, as it seemed he could not force another effort from his leaden arms and legs, his feet struck something hard. Even then the full importance did not drive through his exhaustion-drugged mind. Another stroke carried him into slack water and his knees rasped against the gravel.

Lowering his feet, Mark forced his body erect. Three stumbling strides carried him from the water and then he collapsed, face down on the gravel where he lay without a movement for a long time. Overhead a turkey vulture, circling in search of food, spotted the still shape and dropped closer. No scent of death came from the man, so the black-winged scavenger hovered cautiously. Others of its kind came speeding through the sky, gathering in the way of their kind, to circle over the spot where Mark lay. Finally one of the birds, bolder than the rest, landed on the slope some feet away from the blond giant. Caution held the bird back, but others came drifting down, landing and sitting like evil black statues, waiting for the first scent which would tell them death had come and they might begin their gruesome work in safety.

Overhead the sun shone down, drying Mark's clothes and warming his river-chilled body. Much to the disgust of the gathered turkey vultures, Mark hoisted himself up on his hands. He saw one of the birds, bolder than the rest, had moved towards him. Letting out a startled squawk, the bird flung itself into the air and the remainder of the grisly bunch also took wing, spiralling up but ready to come to earth again.

"You're too early, damn you!" Mark growled, standing up and watching the circling birds. "I'm not ready for you yet."

The rest had done him much good. While he did not feel like repeating the swim, he reckoned he could walk and take care of himself. Throwing another defiant glare at the birds, Mark began to climb the steep wall away from the river.

Night had not quite come as Mark walked through the alley between two buildings which faced Newton's main street. He had entered town from the open country and so far avoided the streets, for he wanted his presence to be unsuspected by Silvie should she still be in town.

A soft footfall sounded behind Mark and he felt something hard, round, familiar, jab into the center of his spine.

"Raise 'em, Ur—" began a male voice.

Instantly Mark acted, although not as the man behind him ordered. From the position of the gun's barrel, he figured its user gripped the butt right-handed and based his moves on that assumption. With a lithe swing, the blond giant pivoted to the right and his off arm lashed back to strike the man's wrist, deflecting the revolver's barrel. Using the same speed which took him to the top ranks of the gunfighting fraternity, Mark brought up his left hand. He clamped hold of the man's right wrist from above with his left hand and held it against his own right forearm in such a way that it could not be turned back into line on him. Before the man had time to make a countermove, Mark's right fist closed its steel-spring strong fingers around bottom of the short-barrelled Merwin & Hulbert Army Pocket revolver and hand which gripped it. A croak of pain came from the man as Mark crushed the trapped hand and he lost his hold of the revolver. With a continuation of the twisting crush which relieved the man of the Merwin gun, Mark sent him pitching over to smash down on his side.

While Mark wondered who the man might be—he wore good quality city clothes, stood six foot with a good if not exceptional build, had a hard, tough, moustached face—there was not time to ask. Even as he threw the man, Mark saw Stash and the other two hard-cases from Mulrooney burst into sight from the rear of the building. Once again Stash reached under his jacket. On the previous occasion he allowed pain to stir his temper and forget the revolver he carried, but did not aim to make the mistake again.

"Hold it," Mark ordered, adopting the deadly efficient gunfighter's crouch and lining the acquired Merwin & Hulbert. "Don't try it. I'm cold, hungry and mean enough to blow your head off."

Stash froze, showing more wisdom than normally, and his two companions halted any moves they might have been planning. While not Western born and raised, they could tell that Mark adopted the move with a speed which told of long practice and the expression on his face warned them that pushing him would be more than hawg-stupid.

"Hey!" yelped the man on the ground, nursing his hand. "You're not Henry Urko."

"I never said I was," Mark answered without relaxing.

"He's still the one who helped Silvie Mainward in Mulrooney, Mr. Wotjac!" Stash pointed out indignantly.

"Why in hell did you do that?" Wotjac demanded hotly.

"You're in no position to start asking," Mark answered.

"Hey now," put in a drawling Texas voice. "What's coming off here?"

Without turning, Mark spoke over his shoulder. "I thought you'd cleaned Newton up so's a man could walk the streets without getting stuck-up, Casey."

"Anybody stupid enough to try to rob you asks for all he gets, Mark," replied Town Marshal Casey Atens, his tall, lean, range-dressed shape backed by a pair of deputies armed with shotguns. "Oh, it's you Wotjac."

"I made a mistake, marshal," Wotjac answered, noting the lack of cordiality in Aten's voice. "When I saw this ja—feller coming through the back of town, I thought he was Henry Urko. It never occurred to me that there might be another man Urko's heft around Newton."

"A man could get killed making fool mistakes like that," drawled Atens. "You look like Sunday morning after a Saturday night's hoo-raw, Mark. What happened to you-all?"

"I could talk better with hot coffee and food in me," Mark replied. "And when I've done, I need the loan of a horse and gun."

"Let's get off the street then," Atens said. "Down at the office'd be as good a place as any for us to talk. I'll have one of the boys fetch you something from the Bijou Cafe."

"I'll come with you marshal—if you don't object," Wotjac put in, changing his tone of demanding as he saw a frown creep to Aten's brow. "This gent might know something that'll help me."

"Come ahead," accepted Atens in a grudging voice. "Mark, this here's Mr. Wotjac of the Pinkerton Agency."

Acknowledging the introduction with no more than a nod, Mark accompanied the marshal's party to the jail and in Atens's office told all that had happened to him. A low-growled curse left Atens's lips and Wotjac let out his breath in a long hiss of annoyance.

"The lil devil!" Atens said. "I've never seen her beat on any stage."

"How's that?" asked Mark.

"She came into town like the devil after a yearling, taking on something fit to go hysterical. When we got her quieted down some she told us how her brother'd been shot and fell into the Fastwater Gorge. I got out there as fast as I could and the sign sure looked that way. So I sent some of the boys who come out with me down below the falls to see if they could find the body. They didn't, but come back with this hat—"

"At least I get something out of it," Mark said, reaching for the hat which Atens lifted from the desk's cupboard.

While the Stetson had lost a couple of the conchas from its band and been battered during its float down river, it still retained its shape. Taking it, Mark found it to be too wet for use and so returned it to the marshal. Wotjac glanced at his men who hovered in the background, clearly wanting to hear more about the girl.

"What did she say happened, I mean who shot her brother?" he said.

"Told me about coming into her uncle's money only some jasper objected to the will and put men after her and her brother," Atens explained. "She seemed real concerned when we didn't find the body, allowed that she might lose the money if we didn't. Made sure we knew that she wasn't too worried over that, but wanted to hope her brother might still be alive. I told her, as easy as I could, that there wasn't much chance of that. Figured his body might have jammed against a rock and maybe come free late. I promised to have men keep watch and brought her back to town. Yes sir, that lil gal sure could act."

"She's not got many to beat, or even come near her in that line," Wotjac admitted. "Silvie Mainward and Henry Urko are about the smartest confidence tricksters the Agency's ever come across."

"Is that why you're after her?" Atens asked.

"Silvie and Urko are the top of their line, like I said. We've three real famous clients wanting them. Urko charms the women and Silvie handles the men and they've took a sizeable fortune at their game. So I've been hunting them, needed extra help and hired these three. They went to Mulrooney while I looked into a rumor that Urko'd been seen in Dodge. Stash allowed that he'd run in with Urko when he met me today and that Silvie and Urko came down here. Which I'd heard, about how he saved that dinger at the depot. That'd be you, Mr. Counter."

"Sure," Mark agreed and glanced at Atens. "Where is she, Casey?"

At that moment the office door opened and a deputy entered, one Mark had not seen before. Atens showed considerable interest in the man, more than a casual reporting in warranted.

"The gal's gone, Casey," the newcomer announced. "Gave me a letter to pass on to you and allowed to be taking the train to Bannock."

"Figured there might be something wrong about the whole deal, even that she put the bullet into her brother," Atens drawled. "So I had Whit here watch her. Only I didn't figure that he'd camp on her door waving his badge."

"Which same I didn't," protested the deputy.

"Don't be too rough on him, marshal," Wotjac put in. "Silvie Mainward's as smart as they come. One time we had an operative watching her. Good man, too, disguised as a blind beggar. She walked over, dropped a dollar in his cup and said, 'Be sure to share it with Allen.'"

"Listen to this," growled Atens, having read the letter while Wotjac spoke and before Mark could inquire whether Allen Pinkerton, current head of the Agency, took a share of the dollar. "She says that she must go to Bannock and see her uncle's lawyer, tell him about her brother's death and will I let her know if we learn anything."

"Like I said," Wotjac grunted. "They don't come any smarter than Silvie. So she's on the train north, deputy?"

"That's what she told me."

"Come on, Stash—"

"Train left maybe fifteen minutes back," Atens drawled.

"Damn it!" Wotjac spluttered. "Why didn't you stop her—"

"Because we didn't know she'd done anything to need stopping for," Atens interrupted. "Maybe if you'd come and told us about her earlier—"

"All right, all right," snorted Wotjac. "We'll go and see if we can get after her some way, boys."

After the Pinkerton men had left the office, the deputy

looked at his marshal with a grin. "Maybe I should've told him—"

"Told him what?" Atens demanded.

"About the gal. She didn't go by train. Sure she went to the depot, but went right on to the livery barn after talking to the ticket man. Took her buggy and lit out. I'd followed her along without her knowing. She left along the old gold mines trail."

Watching Henry Urko load their combined baggage on to the rear of the buggy, Silvie Mainward felt a glow of contentment fill her. Unless she missed her guess, she had succeeded in throwing the Pinkertons off their trail for some time to come. Long enough for herself and Henry to reach the safety of Canada, if to get out of the American continent completely.

A little sigh left the girl as she studied the big, handsome blond man and compared him with Mark "Matson". While Henry might be tall, wide of shoulder and very good looking she had met a man his peer in almost every respect. In a way it was a pity that Mark had to die, although she doubted if he would have possessed the kind of social background to replace Henry. However his death gave Henry and her a chance to escape to a life of leisure on the strength of their illegal gains.

When the United States became too hot to hold them, Silvie—always the brains of the combination—planned their escape. Knowing the tenacity of the Pinkerton Agency, she struck West with Urko, prepared to lay a false scent. While doing so in Mulrooney, she found herself in the hands of Stash's party and received something of a shock when she saw a man she took for Urko coming to her rescue. On realizing that the rescuer was a stranger, Silvie saw possibilities. At first she merely meant to have Mark accompany her to Newton, establish his presence and then send him away. The letter which Mark found at the hotel contained two hundred dollars and a note asking him to meet Silvie at Guthrie in Oklahoma Territory; not that she intended to go there. Unless she missed her guess, a man like "Matson" would not worry unduly over her non-arrival, especially after being well-paid. So he would go his way and lead the Pinkerton men from her. After the display of strength he showed on his arrival, Mark would not soon be forgotten in Newton and the baggage with the semi-obliterated name ought to satisfy any questions as to his identity.

While preparing to leave, Silvie remembered something about the route she must take to meet Henry and changed her plans. If Pinkertons believed Henry to be dead, her problem would be that much easier. She could easily alter appearance so as to be unrecognizable, but that did not apply to Henry. A man of his size stuck out in almost any company. So Mark "Matson" had to die.

Silvie thought back to how the marshal in Newton treated her. Fooled by her acting, he accepted her story and did not even suspect her of killing her "brother"; she regarded the meeting with the deputy as an accident and did not think he might have been watching her. So she felt sure that everything went well. When the body finally appeared, it stood a good chance of being so badly damaged that positive identification would be impossible. In any case, Pinkertons had no photographs to guide them and the body would have to be buried long before they might bring in a witness. Everything had gone just as she hoped it would—

"Silvie!" Urko said urgently, looking past her.

Swinging around, the girl stared in horror at the big man who stepped into view at the end of the building; a cabin erected by some long-forgotten nester but which provided

Urko with a hiding place while she went off to lay the false trail. Although the newcomer wore range clothes, straining the shirt's seams even though it had been the largest size available, had a Colt revolver thrust into his waistband, and held a twin-barrelled ten gauge shotgun in his right hand, Silvie recognized him.

"Y—You!" she gasped.

"Me," agreed Mark Counter.

"Kill him, Henry!" Silvie screamed.

For once Urko did not need her advice. Having heard her story, he recognized Mark and knew there could be only one way out. Nor did he relish the idea of facing the blond giant with bare hands, after hearing of Mark's feat of strength. The big Texan came either for revenge, or in search of Silvie with an idea of a partnership or share of the loot; neither of which appealed to Urko. So he reached for the gun lying on the buggy's seat.

Until he saw the kind of weapon Urko picked up, Mark aimed to take the other without shooting. True Mark came armed, but that had been no more than a precaution. On seeing Urko grab and start to raise the magnificent twin-barrelled twelve gauge shot pistol, Mark knew the precaution paid off. Nor did he offer to meet the threat with the revolver. A man who knew about such matters did not stake his life on a strange handgun and the borrowed Colt served merely as a second line of defense. Faced by another revolver, or Derringer, he would have took his chance on the Colt; but not when the other man gripped a pistol designed to handle shot rather than a solid ball.

Urko started to swing the pistol in Mark's direction, but without the effortless speed of a highly trained gunfighter. Back East he rarely used a weapon and showed some wisdom in selecting one which required little skill in aiming at close range. Unfortunately he faced a man long schooled in such matters and whose life had often depended on speedy reactions.

Gripping the small of the shotgun's butt in his right hand, Mark brought its barrels into line at waist level. There would not even be time to take hold of the foregrip in his left hand, so he did not try. Instead he held the heavy gun one-handed and squeezed the trigger as he sighted by instinctive alignment. Such a way could not offer great accuracy, but that mattered little when using a shotgun. As the barrels kicked up under the right tube's recoil, most of the nine buckshot balls ripped into Urko's body. Even his bulk could not hold off the force of the impact and he jerked backwards. The barrels of his pistol turned and his finger closed on the trigger. Although the pistol roared, its load passed harmlessly by Mark and expended its flight on the open range.

The pistol clattered from Urko's hand as he struck the buggy. Spooked by the sound of the shots, the two horses reared, but they were still secured to the hitching rail and could not escape.

"Henry!" Silvie screamed, throwing herself down at the man's side.

Feet thudded as Atens and a deputy came into sight. They had followed the old trail used by miners on the journey to the Montana gold fields, traveling through the night after Mark fed and caught some needed sleep, checking on the likely hiding places until finding the right one. After what he had been through, Mark claimed the right to go forward first and Atens agreed. Walking forward, the marshal looked at the sobbing girl and the still form by her side.

No matter what was supposed to have happened the previous day, this time one thing was for sure. Henry Urko was now dead.

PART THREE

The Trouble with Wearing Boots

The Ysabel Kid could not help but feel amused when he thought of his current chore. That he should be sent to buy illegally-brewed whisky for a pillar of the Rio Hondo society tickled his sense of humor. Not that Judge Blaze was a hypocrite who publicly condemned moonshiners while secretly purchasing their wares. Like many native Texans, the Judge regarded the Federal Government's demands for tax on whisky as an imposition and infringement of liberty; a law put out by professional politicians who wished to gain the approbation of a very vocal blue-nosed section of the voting public. However the Judge knew that the Kid possessed better qualifications than himself when it came to buying the moonshine. The majority of John County's rural population hailed from the moonshine-brewing mountain country of Kentucky. Like all their kind, they tended to be clannish and suspicious of outsiders. So they required careful handling, but could act friendly enough to a man they regarded as one of their own kind.

Although born in the camp of the Comanche's *Pehnane* band, the Kid could claim that distinction. His maturnal grandfather was Long Walker, chief and war leader of the Dog Soldier lodge, but his father had been a white man of Kentucky blood and kissing-kin to one of the John County families. So the Kid could come and go, within certain bounds, through John County and deal with its people, ensuring that he received only the best of the illicit brews.

A tall, whipcord lean young man, with raven-black hair and a handsome face almost babyishly innocent in appearance, he wore all black clothing from hat to boots. Even his gunbelt bore the same somber hue as it supported an ivory-handled James Black bowie knife sheathed at the left side and a walnut-gripped Colt Dragoon revolver butt forward at his right in a low cavalry twist-draw holster. Ignoring the increased numbers of metal cartridge revolvers offered for sale, the Kid clung to his thumb-busting four pound three ounce hand cannon and swore by its effectiveness in time of war.

Not that the Kid relied entirely upon the Dragoon. Up close he much preferred to exercise his skill with the bowie knife; in the use of which many folks claimed he equaled the designers' ability. Over a distance he called on the services of his magnificent "One of a Thousand" Winchester Model 1873 rifle; won against some of the finest shots in the West at the Cochise County Fair.* In between the two extremes he threw lead from the Dragoon and while not fast—it took him all of a second to draw and shoot, one needed to half that time to be classed as real fast—he could still perform satisfactorily.

A chance observer might have thought the Kid's armament mere ostentation; but not if the onlooker hailed from almost any place west of the Mississippi. Once across the Big Muddy, the Kid's fame spread far over the range coun-

*Told in: *Gun Wizard*.

try. Using the training and lessons learned during his childhood among the Wasps, Quick Stingers, Raiders, whatever one chose to call the *Pehnane*,* the Kid had built a reputation as a master scout and fighting man with few peers. He could follow tracks where a lesser man failed to see a single sign; move in silence no matter how thick, sun-dried or dense the undergrowth; conceal himself in places where one might believe not even a jackrabbit could hide; handle any horse ever foaled; speak several Indian languages and back them with knowledge of each tribe's methods and ways. All in all, the Kid made a friend to be proud of— and a real bad enemy with no exaggerated ideas as to the sanctity of human life.

Few men knew the Rio Grande as did the Kid. Before the Civil War and during it, he rode with his father as a smuggler. When they started up in business for themselves, as opposed to smuggling to aid the Confederate States, Sam Ysabel was murdered in an ambush. While hunting for his father's killers, the Kid met up with Dusty Fog and Mark Counter, accepting their aid to get the men he sought.† With his father dead, the Kid found smuggling no longer held any interest and willingly agreed to become a member of the floating outfit. From being a tough younster following an illegal business which might have one day brought him into conflict with the law, the Kid changed to a highly respected and useful member of the community—although there were people who might have given a stiff argument to *that*.

On arriving in Jack County, the Kid went straight to the home of a trusted old friend; who also sold the best quality

*Told in *Comanche*.

†Told in *The Ysabel Kid*.

"mountain dew" in the area. While old Abel Wallace raised no objections to supplying the Judge with moonshine, he made a request which the Kid could not refuse. A severe attack of rheumatism prevented the old timer from going out to hunt a wild turkey. Being very partial to the succulent flesh of *Meleagris Gallopavo,* Wallace asked the Kid to produce a bird on his behalf. Not averse to eating a slice or two of breast meat from a turkey, especially when cooked as only Granny Wallace could, the Kid readily agreed. However he knew collecting the turkey would be anything but a sinecure.

Hard hunting on the part of the Jack County folks had reduced the numbers of turkeys and those remaining fast developed into smart, constantly alert creatures which taxed a man's ability when he went after them. Already the more stupid birds went under and those remaining bred a strain which knew instinctively of the dangers human beings presented.

There were a number of ways by which a man might find success when hunting even smart turkeys, provided he knew his business thoroughly, although none of them were easy. After due consideration and some discussion with Wallace to learn about local conditions, the Kid decided he would first try stalking a roost-fly-down area. A tom turkey spent its nights in a selected tree—usually a pine in this part of Texas—which offered shelter, a clear view of the surrounding country and a climb no cougar, bobcat or black bear could make without difficulty and warning the bird of its coming. At the first glow of dawn, the tom left its roost-tree and landed in the fly-down area's clearing some hundred or more yards away. After calling up its harem of hens, the tom led them off in a foraging expedition that would cover a fair stretch of country and continue until around noon.

Local knowledge being of vital importance to the hunter,

the Kid questioned Wallace before making a start. Using
the information gathered, he found the tom's roost-tree and
identified it by the droppings and a few feathers lying under
the branches on the ground. From there he moved down
hill, advancing with considerable stealth as he sought for
the roost-fly-down spot. More droppings, tracks and scratch
marks in a clearing which would catch the sun's first warming rays told the Kid he had achieved his end. However he
arrived too late for the birds and moved off already.

"I knew I shouldn't've stayed for that second cup of
coffee," the Kid told himself bitterly and *sotto voce*. "Now
I'll have to do it the hard way."

By which he meant tracking the birds. In later years such
hunting for turkeys classed as top-rate, exacting and demanding sport. The Kid enjoyed matching his wits—as
would many a man who came after him—against the big
birds under those conditions. Scouring the ground with his
eyes, he started to follow the birds' line as they moved
through the woodland in search of fruit, berries, acorns,
nuts, or lizards, grasshoppers and other such living food.
He saw nothing of the actual birds but noticed other tracks.
Whitetail deer, racoon, opossum tracks came before him,
as did the marks left by a big Texas rattlesnake. And there
were wolf tracks, many of them, but they did not surprise
the Kid. While talking about general matters, Wallace mentioned that the wolves were on the increase; so much so
that Ed Solon of the Rafter S had been forced to bring in
a professional wolfer as a safeguard for his cattle.

Time went by without the Kid catching up to the flock
of turkeys. Cautious, silent movement could not be rushed
and he had to ensure that he did not alert the birds too soon.
Towards noon he approached another clearing, one so bare
and uninviting that a less knowledgeable man might have
ignored it as unlikely to interest the turkeys. Knowing better,

the Kid moved forward carefully. Such a spot would be used by the dominant tom of the flock for a strutting area, in which it displayed for the benefit of its harem. In proof the Kid found tracks and arcs torn in the dusty soil by the tom's spread wings. Unfortunately he did not find the birds still absorbed in the strutting performance.

Moving on, the Kid came to the banks of a small stream and found where the flock drank their fill. Unless he missed his guess, he ought to find the birds resting up in a nooning-area close by. Most likely up in the fairly open ground among the tall pine trees on the opposite side of the stream. Yet it would take real careful stalking to approach them.

Before the Kid had covered a hundred yards, he saw the birds. Which did not mean he could start shooting straight away. With a distance of around fifty yards separating them, the Kid could not pick out the bird he wanted or rely on hitting it correctly when selected. Using even greater care, he advanced from cover to cover until he had more than halved the distance and settled down to make his choice.

Studying the birds as they moved about slowly, scratch-ing at the pine-needles underfoot, or stood in the shade thrown by the tree trunks, he located the dominant tom easily. The big bird began to strut, stalking around with fluffed-out feathers, spread and drooping wings, tail fanned out proudly, an act no lesser tom dare adopt in its presence. That told the Kid all he wanted to know even without need-ing to see the tom's foot-long "beard" hanging down. How-ever he did not hunt for a trophy and preferred less leathery and old meat.

Not far from the dominant male stood another tom, younger and with a "beard" less than half the other's size. Yet the young bird carried plenty of meat and so the Kid decided it answered his needs. Carefully he knelt behind the shelter of a pine's trunk and raised his rifle. Not wishing to ruin good meat by hitting the bird's body, he sighted on the head. When sure of his aim, he gently squeezed the Winchester's lightly set trigger.

Startled gobbles rang out as the rifle cracked, then heavy wings drummed as the flock flung themselves into the air. All but the one young tom. Its body bounced up and down, wings beating on the ground, but without a head for that had been shattered by a .44.40 flat-nosed bullet.

Walking forward, the Kid looked down at the dead bird and nodded in satisfaction. Only one thing marred his pleasure at achieving the difficult stalk successfully. Being unable to hunt on horseback, he had left his big white stallion at the Wallace place and so faced a three mile walk while carrying the twenty or more pound turkey. With a grin, he bent down and gripped the bird's legs. Swinging the turkey across one shoulder, he turned and strolled off in the direction of the moonshiner's cabin.

Caution never entirely left the Kid and he still walked with the wary alertness of a much-hunted grizzly bear, watchful but capable of defending himself if the need arose. His eyes constantly darted all-seeing glances about him, noting everything they saw without his needing to think or direct them. After a time he came on to a much-used game path which headed in the required direction and followed it. From the signs, wolves had used the track regularly until a few days before. Not that the Kid worried about them for they would not try to attack a healthy, armed man.

Knowing the need for silent movement, the Kid changed from his high-heeled riding boots to a pair of Comanche moccasins before leaving the cabin. In addition to allowing him to move with the minimum of noise, the moccasins also permitted his feet to feel the ground surface and note its irregularities.

Suddenly the Kid felt the ground under his left foot give

way. Without even a split second's hesitation he jerked the foot up again. So quickly did the Kid react that the closing jaws of a powerful spring trap missed the foot which caused them to operate. Yet it had been a close thing. So close that the jaws' teeth caught and ripped open the sole of the moccasin.

Staggering, the Kid managed to catch his balance and glared at the now-exposed trap. He realized why the wolves had stopped using the trail, although the knowledge did not make him feel any better disposed towards the man who set the trap.

After laying down the turkey and leaning his rifle against the trunk of the nearest tree, the Kid sat down, removed his moccasin and examined the damage. Even a man as tough and unemotional as the Kid could imagine what would have happened had the trap closed its jaws around his ankle. At the worst he might have been crippled for life and certainly would have received a broken bone. Although he avoided injury, he faced the problem of completing the walk to the cabin without his left moccasin's protection.

A faint sound came to his ears, the thudding of horses' hooves. Taking up his rifle, the Kid fired three shots into the air. Clearly whoever rode the horses understood and respected the generally accepted signal of a man needing assistance. After a brief pause, the horses began moving at a better pace and in the Kid's direction. Before long they came into sight, although only one of them carried a rider. Studying the newcomer, a frown flickered on the Kid's face. Maybe the approaching man had been the one who set the trap.

Although not exceptionally tall, the newcomer had breadth to his shoulders and a real powerful frame. Lank black hair hung straggling down from under a battered Stetson hat with an eagle feather thrust into its band. His face bore an even darker tan than the Kid's, while the prominent cheek-bones and aquiline nose hinted at a much greater proportion of Indian blood; the Kid's mother had been half French-Creole. Clearly the man was no cowhand, his buckskin shirt and trousers told that. Bare feet rested in the wooden stirrups of a Comanche saddle, offering further proof that the rider did not work as a cowboy. Around his waist, a belt supported a long-bladed Sommis/Providence bowie knife in a medicine sheath and a walnut-handled Army Colt chambered to take metal cartridges. Across his arm, looking like it grew there, rested a Winchester '73 rifle, its woodwork decorated by brass tacks. He sat afork a bay horse of Indian breeding and led a second which carried a tarpaulin-wrapped pack.

An angry grunt came from the man as he brought his horses to a halt and looked down at the exposed trap, then he raised his eyes to the Kid.

"It get you, *Chuchilo?*" he asked in a deep-throated voice and using the Kid's *Pehnane* man-name although the rest of his speech was in English.

"Near on," replied the Kid coldly. "Did you put it there?"

"Me?" the man snorted, showing indignation. "Barefoot Joe don't do a fool-stupid thing like that. I don't need store-bought traps to kill wolves."

While the Kid had heard of Barefoot Joe, he did not know the man. Barefoot Joe made his living by roaming the range country and hunting down stock-killing animals. Being half Comanche—his mother had been a member of the *Tanima,* Liver-Eaters band—he learned the ways of wild animals as part of his schooling and proved very successful without needing to purchase metal traps as an aid to his work.

"Somebody planted it," drawled the Kid.

"Yeah. And it shouldn't be here," Barefoot Joe went on. "This's Rafter S range and Solon took me on to get rid of the wolves."

"Could be that somebody else aims to cut in on your game."

"Not know much about wolves, whoever he is," sniffed Joe. "I bet he left his scent along here. Something sure scared them wolves from coming along the path."

"And about the time that damned trap was planted," the Kid agreed.

"Where you headed, *Cuchilo?*" Joe inquired, bending to pluck the trap from the ground.

"Over to the Wallace place. I've just shot a turkey for Abel."

"You'd best ride the pack hoss then and I'll take you over there. I'm going to Jack City, got some good wolf skins to sell at store."

"Thanks, Joe," the Kid accepted and swung astride the pack horse despite being loaded with the rifle and turkey. "Lord, I sure hate walking."

"You should stop wearing them boots," Joe told him. "They sure cramp a man's feet something fierce."

A grin flickered across the Kid's face. "You could be right at that."

On reaching the Wallace cabin, the Kid found that he could not sit back and relax while waiting for the arrival of the cooked bird. Although Granny aimed to start work straight away, it would be some time before the turkey came on to the table. She asked the Kid if he would ride into Jack City and collect some cloth ordered by selection from a dreambook; the catalogue of an Eastern mail-order company. While he went, Abel could attend to bottling the Judge's whisky and Granny get on unhindered with her cooking, so the Kid agreed to go. Donning his boots, he collected and saddled the magnificent white stallion he used as a personal mount. With the horse between his knees, the Kid accompanied

Barefoot Joe towards Jack City.

Although bearing the title "City", the seat of John County was merely a typical small town of the Texas range country. Its business section spread in an untidy straggle along the main, and only, street and the homes of its citizens dotted the area without any attempt at civic planning. Leaving Joe at the general store, the Kid rode on and came to a halt at the Wells Fargo depot which also served as a post office. He learned that Granny's order had not yet arrived, but that it might be on the stage which should be coming in soon. Settling down on one of the seats placed outside the office for the benefit of customers, passengers, or anybody who might feel like taking a rest, the Kid chatted with the agent and waited for the stage to come.

Jack City was quiet and restful in the cool of the late afternoon. Peaceful too, although it had once been in the grip of an Eastern criminal and his gang. Now the town no longer lived in fear, due to the efforts of the floating outfit,* as the Wells Fargo agent remarked.

Then the peace ended. Suddenly the door of the general store burst open and its owner, a small, mild man with a reputation for fair dealing and honesty, dashed out in a state of considerable agitation.

"Help!" he yelled. "Help, there's trouble inside!"

In corroboration to his words, shouts, crashes and thuds sounded from inside the building. The Kid left his seat, vaulting the hitching rail to land at the side of his stallion. Sliding the rifle from its saddleboot, he ran along the street towards the store. Before he reached the building, a man crashed through one of its windows taking both glass and sash with him. More noise came from the inside and the evicted man landed on the sidewalk.

*Told in *Law of the Gun*.

The Kid thrust open the store's front door and stepped hurriedly aside as a second man came rushing in his direction. As the man came backwards and passed by with no reduction of pace, it could be assumed that he did not do so of his own free will. Blood ran from his nose and his face showed pain as he went past the Kid to continue until he fell from the sidewalk and landed on his rump in the street.

Ignoring the man, the Kid entered the store and looked around. On the counter lay Barefoot Joe's rifle and the tarpaulin pack open to show a number of prime wolf skins. The cracker barrel had been overturned, its contents trampled underfoot but the large flour barrel at the other end of the counter still stood upright. Although the Kid noted such details, his main attention centered on the left wall. There stood Barefoot Joe, one hand bunching the lapels of a fat, scared-looking man's city-style jacket, forcing him against the wall and the other hand slid the long blade of the Sommis bowie knife from its sheath.

"Try to cheat and rough-handle Barefoot Joe, would you?" yelled the hunter.

One glance told the Kid all he needed to know. If he could not guess at just how the trouble started, the words gave him some clue. Yet Benjiman, the owner of the store, was a man noted for his honesty. Putting aside his interest in what caused the trouble, the Kid set about ending it as quickly as he could. Unless he brought Joe's actions to a halt, the hunter might do something drastic and far more permanent than knocking a man through the door or window.

Stopping Barefoot Joe posed something of a problem. Only a fool would try to *talk* him into a more amenable frame of mind and the Kid was not stupid enough to make so futile an attempt.

Advancing as silently as he could manage with a coating of spilled crackers underfoot, the Kid approached Barefoot Joe from the hunter's rear. Despite the soft-footed advance, Joe heard him coming and swung around. However the hunter made a mistake. He turned ready to meet a renewed attack from one of the white men and at such a moment the Kid moved with all the deadly speed of a full-blooded Comanche. More than that, the Kid knew that he faced another member of the *Nemenuh** and acted accordingly. Around and up swung the Kid's rifle, making a smooth arc which drove its metal-shod butt hard against the side of Joe's jaw. Taken off balance by the force of the blow, Joe pitched sideways. His knife clattered from his hand and he crashed to the floor.

"Sorry, Joe," the Kid apologized. "But I wasn't taking chances with y—"

Freed from Joe's hand, the fat man spluttered curses and dipped his hand into a pocket. Swinging around, the Kid saw a Remington Double Derringer coming into sight and also heard feet thudding through the store's door behind him. A quick taken glance showed him that the man knocked through the door had re-entered and clearly aimed to take cards in the game once more. Dressed in range clothes and belting a low-tied Colt, the man looked like the type of drifter who loafed around Western towns and took any work which did not entail undue raising of sweat, or willingly became involved in any fuss if he thought doing so might profit him. With his face twisted in rage, blood dribbling down from his nostrils still, he rushed in the direction of the sprawled-out, dazed hunter and reached for his gun as he went.

As usual the Kid acted fast and effectively. Thrusting

*Nemenuh: "The People", the Comanche's name for themselves.

the rifle forward, he drove its barrel with considerable force into the pit of the fat man's stomach. Agony twisted the man's face, his fingers opened and let the Derringer clatter to the floor and he clutched at his injured mid-section.

From taking the fat jasper out of the fight, the Kid gave his attention to dealing with the other. Once again he figured that mere words would not change the man in question's mind and so wasted no time in trying. Twisting around, the Kid removed his left hand from the rifle's foregrip. With his right hand still on the small of the butt, the Kid swung the rifle around and up. While the advancing man saw his danger, he could not halt his forward rush. The barrel of the rifle lashed forward and maced into his throat. Dropping his revolver, the lean man staggered back gagging and croaking, tripped and landed hard on his rump once more.

Directing his gaze towards the fat man again, the Kid found him recovered sufficiently from the jab in the belly to make an attempt at picking up the Derringer.

"Leave it lie!" ordered the Kid, slapping the Winchester's foregrip back into his waiting left hand and slanting its barrel in the fat man's direction.

People appeared at the front door, peering inside and talking among themselves. Then the crowd parted, making way for Tony Blevins, town marshal and county sheriff combined in one leathery old timer as lean as arrow-weed and tough as they came. While Blevins might ignore the activities of the county's moonshiners, he was a honest lawman and had been brought in after the floating outfit cleaned the Eastern gang from the region.

"What's coming off here, Kid?" Blevins inquired, darting glances around the room. "Looks like there's been some tolerable fuss going on."

"You might say that," the Kid replied.

At which point the fat dude thrust himself indignantly

from the wall. He was a fairly tall, heavily-built man with a surly, loose-lipped face that perspired easily. Clad in good quality city clothes, a suit of the latest Eastern style, and giving off an affluent air, he reminded the Kid of more objectionable Easterners such as one came across in the Kansas trail-end towns. If the dude should be a citizen of long standing around John County, he had never been there when the Kid made a visit.

"Do your duty, sheriff!" the dude ordered in the tone of an influential taxpayer addressing a humble peace officer whose salary he helped to pay.

"Which's why I come here, Mr. Schweitzer," Blevins answered evenly.

A deep grunt from Barefoot Joe drew all eyes in his direction. Sitting up on the floor, he felt gently at his jaw. Then he shook his head and started to rise.

"Huh!" he grunted. "You hit hard, *Cuchilo*."

"I didn't reckon you'd listen to reason any other way," drawled the Kid.

"Most likely I wouldn't have," admitted the hunter and bent to pick up his knife. "Them fellers got me plenty mad."

"Stop him!" screeched Schweitzer, staring as Joe rose holding his knife.

"Don't you go raising a muck-sweat, Mr. Schweitzer," Blevins replied. "I don't figure that Joe here aims to use it for whittling his name on the counter."

"He won't even use it on you," the Kid went on.

"Maybe I should," growled Joe, scowling at Schweitzer as he slipped the Sommis bowie back into its sheath. "Him one big cheat. Offer me half what them skins worth and had them two fellers jump me when I said I wanted to see Benjiman."

"It's a lie!" Schweitzer yelled. "These damned half-breeds—"

The words ended as the Kid's rifle thrust gently into Schweitzer's throat, although there was nothing gentle in his red-hazel eyes as he studied the dude.

"My grandpappy's Chief Long Walker of the *Pehname* Comanche, *hombre*," the Kid said quietly. "I didn't hear right what you just said."

"Ease off, Kid," suggested Blevins. "Mr. Schweitzer didn't mean nothing by it. Did you, Mr. Schweitzer?"

For a moment Schweitzer tried to meet the Kid's hostile gaze and failed badly. Somehow all the babyish innocence had left the dark features, to be replaced by a cold Comanche Dog Soldier's mask which drove shivers through the dude despite his never having seen one of those very able warriors in war or peace.

"I—I didn't mean anything," Schweitzer answered, trying to hide his hate. He failed and the Kid knew Schweitzer would not soon forget the incident.

"We'd best hear your side of it, Mr. Schweitzer," Blevins said, then his eyes swung to where the lean man had wriggled around and was reaching for the revolver dropped when the Kid's rifle landed. "Leave it lie there, Totnes. You don't need it for anything."

While Totnes might have liked to give the sheriff an argument about that, he knew better than do so. Granted that Totnes had Schweitzer's backing, but the fat man did not yet have sufficient influence in town to override the sheriff's authority. Nor would Blevins allow such a thing to prevent him doing his duty. So the lean man rose, his hand massaging his sore throat, and contented himself with sharing glares of hatred between the Kid and Barefoot Joe.

The crowd scattered as the second of Barefoot Joe's attackers came charging in. Big, burly, wearing range clothing and the rig of a fast man with a gun, Buck Plaid returned with the intention of continuing the assault on Barefoot Joe.

However he changed his mind when he saw the sheriff looking in his direction. While Plaid had several citizens of Jack City buffaloed, Tony Blevins was not among them. So Plaid halted and darted a glance at Schweitzer as if seeking for information and advice on how he should act. After the one quelling look at Plaid, Blevins turned to Schweitzer once more and repeated his request.

"There must have been some mistake, sheriff," Schweitzer replied, scowling a little. He might have been raised back East, but had lived in Texas long enough to know a man did not use the word "mister" when addressing a liked or respected acquaintance.

"What kind of mistake?" Blevins wanted to know.

"This ha—" began Schweitzer and stopped as he saw a slight tightening of the Kid's lips. The rifle's muzzle had left his throat, but still hung before its owner ready for use. "This feller came in with his skins and I offered him a fair price. He got mean and reckoned it wasn't enough. Mr. Plaid and Mr. Totnes came to try and reason with him, but he attacked them."

"Only he reasoned back faster than they could," drawled the Kid.

"This's no joking matter!" snorted Schweitzer. "Look at the damage he did."

"How come Joe offered you the skins?" asked the Kid. "This Eli Benjiman's store, ain't it?"

"I'm his partner," Schweitzer explained.

Looking around, Blevins saw Benjiman standing at the forefront of the crowd and asked him what started the trouble.

"I'm not sure," Benjiman answered, throwing a cold glance at his partner. "I was working in the back when I heard the fuss, came out, saw what was happening and came to fetch help."

"You didn't hear what was said in here then?"

"Not a word of it, Tony. The wall's fairly thick and I didn't hear anything until somebody or something crashed into it."

"These two men heard and saw everything," Schweitzer pointed out. "Why not ask them?"

"I'll get around to it, Mr. Schweitzer," Blevins promised.

"Barefoot Joe tell you truth, sheriff," the hunter put in.

"I've got to hear all sides, Joe," Blevins answered. "How about it, Plaid?"

"The breed jumped Mr. Schweitzer for nothing," answered the big hard-case.

"He sure did," backed up Totnes.

"That's a damn big l—" Joe growled and reached towards his knife's hilt.

"Take it easy, Joe," the Sheriff ordered and the hunter relaxed. "What got it all started, Mr. Plaid?"

Clearly Plaid felt undecided on how he should answer the question. He looked first at Totnes then towards Schweitzer as if in search of inspiration.

"Me 'n' Buck—" Totnes began.

"Let Plaid tell it," interrupted the sheriff. "You'll have your turn later."

Brief though the respite had been, it gave Plaid the time needed to think up a reason for not being able to hand out more exact information. A glow of satisfaction came to his face and he threw a reassuring glance towards Schweitzer.

"I was over there, looking at the guns and had my back to them. When I heard the breed yelling, I turned round. There he was, hauling Mr. Schweitzer over the counter with his knife in his hand."

"So me 'n' Buck come over to try and quieten him down peaceable," Totnes went on hurriedly. "Only the breed jumped us—"

"It's surely a pleasure to meet public-spirited gents like you pair," the Kid put in. "Where'd ole Joe cut you?"

"Cut us?" repeated Totnes, frowning in a puzzled manner.

"With his knife," defined the Kid.

"I don't get it," Totnes answered.

"Mister, happen you'd've jumped Joe while he held a knife, you'd've got it all right. Plumb up to its hilt in your favorite belly."

"What're you getting at, Kid?" asked Blevins.

"Funny feller ole Joe there," drawled the Kid. "He's hauling his *hombre* here," he jerked a thumb in Schweitzer's direction, "over the counter with one hand and getting set to whittle his head to a sharp point with a knife in the other. Then when he gets jumped by two public-spirited fellers, he shoves the knife back into its sheath and fights 'em off with his hands."

"How's that?" growled Blevins.

"The knife was in its sheath when I come in here," the Kid told him and gave the three men a challenging look.

Speculation showed on Blevin's face as he thought over the implications of the Kid's statement. If the Kid spoke the truth, which Blevins did not doubt, Joe started the fight empty-handed. Both the hard-cases had been outside the store before the Kid entered, and it seemed unlikely that Barefoot Joe would draw his knife to threaten Schweitzer, sheath it when attacked by the two men, only to pull it once more.

With that thought in mind, Blevins looked to where Joe's rifle lay on the counter. That too held a certain significance. Attacked by two men, he ought to have used the rifle to defend himself.

All in all Blevins felt far from happy at what he saw. He faced a difficult predicament, one on which his future in Jack City might depend. After only a short time in residence, Schweitzer had gained popularity among a section of the population which wielded much influence. Blevins knew that his appointment as sheriff had not been universally popular and his ways of handling the law did not suit everybody in town. Handled wrongly, the affair could give Blevins's opposition a chance to move him from office.

One thing the sheriff knew. He would be highly unlikely to learn the truth of the business in a way that suited all parties involved.

"I demand that you arrest this man, sheriff!" Schweitzer stated in a loud voice, seeing that a few of his influential friends hovered in the background. "He's not safe to be roaming the streets."

"Joe's been here more than once and roamed 'em without hurting anybody," Blevins answered.

"I've never had any trouble with him," Benjiman went on, glaring in a hostile manner at his partner.

"Likely he never had cause to make any afore today," drawled the Kid.

"What's that mean?" growled Schweitzer.

"Wolf hunting's hard and risky work, mister. A man wouldn't take to having somebody trying to pay him half of what the skins're worth."

"I tell you that I made him a fair offer!"

"He says he give three dollar a skin," Joe interrupted. "Benjiman always pay six. When I ask to see Benjiman, this fat *hombre* tell them two to throw me out. Only Barefoot Joe don't throw that easy."

"That's for sure," grinned the Kid, thinking of how Plaid went through the window and Totnes passed out of the door.

"What're you going to do, marshal?" Schweitzer snapped.

"Just what do you want me to do, Mr. Schweitzer?" countered Blevins.

"I demand the protection of the law!"

"Which same you've got."

"Are you going to arrest him?"

"For what?" Blevins asked mildly.

"Assaulting me—" began Schweitzer.

"Sure. But I'll have to take you three as well."

"For what reason?"

"Assaulting him back."

"But that's ridiculous!" snorted Schweitzer.

"Why?" asked Blevins. "Those two jaspers jumped him, even if they did get the worst of it. Maybe I won't be able to arrest you, but I'm taking them two in."

A single glance warned Schweitzer that the two men did not relish the idea of being taken to jail. Unless he wanted them to change their stories radically, he must prevent the sheriff from carrying out the threat.

"If that's how you see your duty," sheriff," he said, "there's nothing I can do. However, rather than cause these men any inconvenience, I'm willing to drop the charges against the ha—hunter."

"Happen you do that, I reckon Joe'll not want anything more doing," Blevins replied with a dry grin.

"But there's the matter of the damage done to our property," Schweitzer pointed out and indicated the overturned cracker barrel.

"You figure that Joe should pay for it, mister?" asked the Kid.

"I don't figure on anything, young man," Schweitzer answered for he had seen Cyrus Rascover, the local justice-of-the-peace, standing among the crowd. "I am willing to allow the law to make that decision."

Sensing a chance to increase a potentially influential citizen's friendship, Rascover entered the room. At the sight of the middle-sized, stocky and soberly-dressed figure,

Blevins barely managed to stifle a groan. If Rascover exercised his official rights, only a cast-iron case would save Barefoot Joe. The justice-of-the-peace would be sure to favor Schweitzer and the storekeeper had two witnesses in his favor. However there was no way in which Blevins could prevent Rascover from taking a hand in what had now become a civil rather than criminal legal action.

"I think this matter can be settled legally," Rascover announced in his most pompous manner. "In fact I am willing to open the court tomorrow at noon and hear both sides before handing down a decision."

"Tomorrow will suit me fine, your honor," said Schweitzer in an ingratiating tone.

"I got work to do, can't hang around here," Barefoot Joe objected.

"You'll appear before the court or be held in default!" Rascover barked.

"Not have time to waste. I told truth and that's all."

"If you don't appear. I'll find against you!"

"He can do it, too, Joe," warned the Kid.

"Then me take skins and go," the hunter replied.

"The skins stay here, their value being held as bail to ensure your return," Rascover corrected.

"Easy, Joe!" ordered the Kid as he saw the anger which twisted the other's face. "He can do that and have the law behind him. You'll have to do as he says."

"Can't leave trap until noon tomorrow, *Cuchilo*," Joe answered. "Other animals maybe spoil skin of one caught unless I get it out."

"You figuring to stop this gent making his living, judge?" the Kid asked. "'Cause if so, he'll need a lawyer. I reckon I can get to the OD Connected afore Temple Houston leaves and I reckon he'll act for Joe happen Ole Devil asks him."

"Ole Devil?" repeated Rascover. "Is he interested in this business?"

"He will be when I tell him about it."

Worry lines creased Rascover's brow at the Kid's reply. While Schweitzer might be an up-and-coming citizen of Jack City, it would be many years—if ever—before he reached the State-wide prominence of Ole Devil Hardin. Nor could Rascover plead ignorance to Temple Houston's identity as son of the great Sam Houston and one of Texas's leading lawyers. Houston often visited the OD Connected, being a welcome friend and would be willing to lend his not inconsiderable aid if requested. So, while eager to keep Schweitzer's friendship, Rascover did not wish to do so at the expense of antagonizing either Ole Devil or Temple Houston. The situation called for quick thinking, tact and diplomacy; all of which Rascover felt he possessed in large quantities.

"Naturally it isn't this court's intention to imperil any citizen's livelihood," he stated. "If Mr.—"

"Barefoot Joe," supplied the Kid.

"If Mr. Barefoot Joe will leave his skins in the hands of the sheriff as a sign of good faith, I see no reason why he shouldn't attend to his business and return in time to attend court."

"He won't have time," the Kid pointed out.

"Then we will change the time until six o'clock tomorrow evening," said Rascover amiably.

"That do you, Joe?" asked Blevins.

"What you think, *Cuchilo?*"

"I'd do it, was I you, Joe."

"It's all right with me then," Joe stated. "You good friend, not lead Barefoot Joe wrong."

"I surely hope that I don't," drawled the Kid. "Let's go."

While the business had not gone entirely as he hoped, Schweitzer could see no way of changing things. However he might be able to utilize the added time by making sure that Rascover saw the benefits of continued friendship. With evidence of three against one and a favorable judge handling the action, all should go—

The thought ended as Schweitzer found his partner standing before him and saw the anger on the other's face.

"I want a word with you in the back room," Benjiman stated grimly.

"Certainly, that's what partners are for," smiled Schweitzer glancing to where the marshal wrapped up Joe's skins. "Come on."

Passing through the crowd and on to the street with Barefoot Joe at his side, the Kid saw no sign of the stagecoach but the Wells Fargo agent came over to him.

"Just got word from Diggers Wells, Kid. The stage won't be here until early tomorrow morning. I telegraphed and asked about Granny's parcel and they say it's aboard."

"Then I'll come in early and pick it up for her," the Kid promised. "I'll ride a ways with you, Joe."

"Hey, Kid," called Blevins, leaving the store with the tarp slung on his shoulder. "Is Temple Houston over to the OD Connected?"

"Nope," replied the Kid.

"Lying to the judge for shame," grinned Blevins. "I thought you Injuns always told the truth?"

"I'm only part Injun," drawled the Kid, unabashed. "Get the lying from the white side of the family."

Holding his big white stallion to a steady walk, the Kid rode into Jack City early on the next morning. After enjoying Granny's turkey, he spent the night at the Wallace place and left before daylight. He wanted to collect Granny's parcel so as not to delay his return to the Rio Hondo unduly. Most likely there would be other work awaiting him and even if not he knew his friends aimed to spend Saturday night in Diggers Wells, so wished to accompany them.

Only a few people were about as the Kid rode into town. Along by the Wells Fargo office men worked at unloading the stagecoach and changing its team. The sheriff ambled down towards his office ready to start another day's work. As the Kid approached, Schweitzer appeared through the alley by the store and turned along its front without even glancing in the dark Texan's direction.

The shattered window of the store had been covered with planks of wood to prevent anybody entering during the night, but it seemed that the precaution failed. Halting, Schweitzer stared at the edge of the window and then stepped forward to draw away the planks. Nails rose from the inner sides of the planks, showing that they had been secured to the wall, but they no longer held in place. With the planks pulled aside, Schweitzer gave a startled yell and stepped back hurriedly. Then he turned and dashed along the street towards the sheriff's office.

"Murder!" he screeched. "Murder! Help, sheriff!"

Showing surprising speed for a man who would never see fifty again, Blevins loped along to meet the running man. Other people appeared at doors, the men by the stage halted their work and every eye held on the fat shape of the storekeeper as he and the sheriff came to a stop facing each other. Sending his horse forward at a better pace, the Kid approached and could hear Schweitzer's words.

"I—It's Eli Benjiman, sheriff. He's lying by the counter with his throat cut from—"

Without waiting to hear more, the sheriff pushed by Schweitzer and ran in the direction of the store. Relief flickered on Blevins's seamed old face as he saw the Kid and he growled a request for the other to come along. Should there have been murder done, Blevins might require the services of a man famous for his skill at reading sign. In his day Blevins bore such a reputation, but age took the keen edge from his eyes and he knew the Kid could handle such a chore better than himself.

On reaching the store, the Kid dropped from his saddle and sent the stallion walking off along the street to halt before the next building. Tied or loose, the horse could be relied upon to stay put until needed, but leaving it outside the store presented difficulties. At best Blackie only barely tolerated strangers and the Kid did not intend chancing leaving his horse to be in the center of a milling, excited crowd.

When sure there would be no danger to the citizens of Jack City through too close contact with Blackie, the Kid swung on to the sidewalk and joined Blevins. The sheriff drew away the loose planks and looked inside. One glance told him all he needed to know. Peering over Blevins's shoulders, the Kid could see a pair of legs emerging from behind the counter and that the flour barrel had been overturned, its contents making a large spread of whiteness on the floor.

"Let's get in, Kid," the sheriff said.

They went to the door and Blevins twisted its handle. Nothing happened.

"It's still locked most likely," Schweitzer said, coming up. "When I saw the window had been forced, I looked in and didn't wait to try the door."

"Open her up then," Blevins ordered.

Taking a key from his pants pocket, Schweitzer inserted it into the hole, or tried as it would not go far.

"Eli's key's in the lock on the other side," he told the waiting men.

"I'll go through the window, Tony," the Kid offered and Blevins nodded his agreement.

By pulling on the planks, the Kid found he could easily enter through the window. Much as he wished to look around, he first crossed to and unlocked the door. Blevins entered, followed by Schweitzer, and headed for the counter. Apparently he had given orders to the crowd, for they hovered around on the sidewalk but none tried to enter.

"It's Eli all right," said the sheriff in a strained voice.

Even after a lifetime spent enforcing law in Texas, he found the sight that met his eyes to be sickening. Benjamin's body lay on its back, stiff and still. Clad only in a collarless shirt, trousers and socks, the body looked ghastly due to the amount of blood which had poured from the deep slash that laid bare the throat almost to the bone.

"Look here!" hissed Schweitzer in a dramatic tone, pointing down to the spilled flour. "Footprints."

Although he had seen them on entering, the Kid left examining the footprints until after unlocking the door. Walking to Schweitzer's side, he looked down.

"They sure are," confirmed the Kid.

"Made by bare feet!" Schweitzer went on.

"Yep," agreed the Kid.

"That damned half-breed doesn't wear shoes. And I saw him coming through town late last night."

"When was this?" asked Blevins.

"Late on. Past midnight," Schweitzer replied. "I couldn't sleep and was walking up and down my room. Looked out of the window and saw him riding by."

"You sure it was Barefoot Joe?" the Kid said.

"Real sure. I'll not forget him easy," Schweitzer answered, then a thought seemed to strike him and leaned across the counter. "The cash drawer's out and been emptied. Damn it, sheriff, if you'd held that—"

"How'd you know Joe did it?" asked the Kid.

"Who else around here goes barefoot?" snapped Schweitzer. "It was that damned half-breed hunter."

A low growl of anger rose from the listening crowd and Barefoot Joe's name ran from mouth to mouth. No matter how the citizens might regard Schweitzer, Benjiman was universally liked and respected around town. So his murder aroused a feeling of hatred against the killer.

"Now hold hard there, Mr. Schweitzer," drawled Blevins. "We don't know for sure it was Barefoot Joe who did it."

"Then why was he back in town last night?' demanded the storekeeper hotly. "He must have come back looking for me, bust in here and disturbed Eli. You can see there's been a struggle in here, that flour barrel didn't tip over without help. When he killed Eli, he emptied the cash drawer and got the hell out of it."

At that moment, an old man entered. While employed as a swamper at the saloon, he augmented a meager salary by cleaning out the sheriff's office and jail.

"You been down the office this morning, Tony?" the old man asked.

"No. Why?"

"Safe door's open. I know it don't lock, but you allus close it. Was there anything in it?"

"Yeah," said Blevins. "That bundle of skins I was holding."

"Well they ain't there now," the swamper informed him. "That safe's as empty as a skinflint's cupboard when you go calling."

"There!" shouted Schweitzer. "Do you need more proof, sheriff? He came back after those skins and saw his chance to get even with me at the same time."

"It looks like that Barefoot Joe *hombre* fooled us complete, Tony," the Kid growled.

"I'm—" Blevins began.

"I know just how you feel," the Kid interrupted. "It riles me to think that he fooled me, too."

"Then what do you aim to do about it?" spat Schweitzer.

"I'm going right after him and aim to bring him in," stated the Kid and looked hard at the sheriff. "It's no use you trying to talk me out of going, neither, Tony. I know my right and true civic duty."

"Maybe the breed won't want to come in," Schweitzer suggested.

"Then I'll just have to fetch him," answered the Kid.

"He'll fight."

"If I give him the chance."

"Why not take some help with you?" asked the storekeeper.

"There's not a hoss in this whole country that can keep up with my ole Blackie," answered the Kid. "So I'll go alone. I can handle any liver-eating *Tanima* and I'll fetch him in even if it's across his saddle."

"I'll give you five hundred dollars no matter how you bring him in," Schweitzer promised in a broken voice. "Eli was a real good man who never did harm to anybody and I want to see the man who killed him—"

"You'll do that, mister," promised the Kid.

With that, he turned and walked out of the store. For a moment Blevins stood staring in a disbelieving manner and then stumped angrily after the Kid. Catching up with the Indian-dark youngster as he reached the side of the white stallion, Blevins scowled at him.

"Just what the hell's your game, Kid?" the sheriff asked.

"Like I said in there, I'm fixing to fetch Joe in."

"For the reward?"

"Pappy allus used to tell me that money didn't buy happiness, sheriff," the Kid drawled. "But it sure helps a man be miserable real comfortable."

"You saw the sign in there," Blevins growled.

"Why sure," agreed the Kid. "Which same's why *I'm* fixing to fetch Joe in. See you when I get back, Tony. I reckon you'll be able to find plenty to do here in town 'til then."

Holding his horse to a fast trot which ate miles, the Kid rode through the John County rangeland. He followed a trail carved by the wheels of a chuckwagon and hooves of a number of horses, heading in the direction of the Rafter S ranch. On the previous evening he had parted company with Barefoot Joe, the other returning to the ranch, so thought that it ought to be a good place to make a start. While riding, the Kid kept a watch on his back trail but saw nothing to worry him.

Two hours later he came into sight of the ranch house and noticed Joe's saddle-horse standing before it. Riding closer, the sound of Blackie's hooves brought two men from the house and they halted on the porch looking in the Kid's direction. Although Barefoot Joe looked amiable, the tall, tanned man at his side showed no such emotion. Cold-eyed, with his hand hanging negligently close to the butt of his low-hanging Peace-maker, Ed Solon studied the Kid with interest and then gave the surrounding range a quick scrutiny.

"Howdy, Joe," greeted the Kid, halting his horse but remaining in the saddle until he should be invited to dismount.

"What brings you over this way, Kid?" Solon inquired before Joe could reply.

"I came to take Joe into town."

"He told me about that fuss there and I'm not so sure he should go back."

"I reckon he'd best come," said the Kid.

"Why?" asked the rancher. "Light and rest your saddle."

Swinging down, the Kid left his horse standing range tied, the trailing reins being sufficient to hold it still. Then he told the two men what had happened in town the previous night and finished by asking Joe a question.

"Where'd you spend the night?"

"Here," growled Solon.

"His hoss's been rid and the tracks I saw back there showed he's only just come in," the Kid pointed out.

"So?" challenged the rancher.

"How about it, Joe?" asked the Kid, ignoring Solon.

"Me got after them wolves and stopped out all night. Shot five and skinned 'em. Then went round traps to see what I'd caught."

"You'd best come in town and tell that to the sheriff," suggested the Kid.

"You don't have to go with him, Joe," Solon stated.

"He'll come happen he knows what's best for him," the Kid replied.

"You reckon you can take him?" Solon growled.

"I tell you one thing," drawled the Kid. "I surely aim to try."

"Just you?"

"I don't want the rest of the floating outfit to have to cut in."

Once more Solon's eyes raked the surrounding area. Suddenly he became painfully aware that men could hide in a number of places within rifle range, especially if they possessed the kind of fighting ability credited to the members of the floating outfit.

"Was they there, it's be Cap'n Fog doing the talking," the rancher finally decided.

"I never said Dusty was here," the Kid answered. "But that don't count for Waco, or Doc Leroy."

While not quite so well known as Dusty Fog or Mark Counter, the two men named rapidly gained prominence due to their membership in the floating outfit. Both could be relied upon to back any play the Kid made, if they happened to be hid out close by. Which brought up a point; were they lying in cover, looking along the barrels of their rifles?

"There's no need for fuss, Ed," Barefoot Joe announced. "Me trust *Cuchilo* and reckon he knows what he's doing."

"Maybe I ought to bring a few of the boys along—" began Solon.

"That'd make sure that folks thought Joe'd done it," the Kid answered, knowing that the Rafter S did not have the best of reputations around Jack City.

"Me go alone," Joe stated. "Not have anything to be scared of."

"Play it your way then," grunted Solon and looked at the Kid with cold eyes. "Mind that he gets treated fair, Kid."

"I'll see he does," the Kid promised and walked to his horse.

While riding away from the ranch, Joe turned and grinned at the Kid.

"You make a good bluff, *Cuchilo*. Me know that you got no *amigos* hid out."

"Solon didn't," replied the Kid.

After that, neither of them talked much; no Comanche

did when traveling. However they kept their eyes constantly
on the move and missed nothing that went on around them.
Riding through the rough, broken country about two miles
from town, with a gentle breeze blowing into their faces,
the Kid seemed to be completely relaxed and at ease. So
much so that he lifted his pleasant tenor voice in song.

"The judge said, 'Stand up, boy, and dry off your tears,
  You're going to prison for twenty-one years,'
So kiss me goodbye, love, and say you'll be mine.
For twenty-one years is a mighty long time.
Three months've gone by, love, I wish I was dead,
This dirty ole jail-house, the floor is my bed,
It's raining and pouring, the moon shows no light,
Oh, honey, please tell me why you never write.
I counted the days, Love, I counted the nights,
I counted the footsteps, I counted the lights,
I've counted the clouds, and I've counted the stars,
And I've counted all of these prison bars.
Six months have gone by now and no letter came,
A year has passed and it's still the same,
For love of a woman, I fell into crime,
And twenty-one years is a mighty long ti—"

   Suddenly the white stallion threw up its head and let out
an explosive snort which ended the Kid's song. It looked
just like some magnificent wild animal that had caught a
warning scent and sounded the alarm. Instantly the Kid fell
sideways and to the left out of his saddle. While falling, he
caught and slid free the Winchester from the saddleboot.
On landing, he rolled from the trail and into the shelter
offered by a large rock. Carefully the rifle raised, cuddling
its butt into his shoulder and his right eye squinted along
the barrel. He fired two shots spacing them about a foot

about so that their bullets tore through a clump of mesquite some eighty yards away.

Even as the Kid left his saddle, Barefoot Joe also dropped to the ground and dived behind the stunted trunk of a nearby scrub oak, from where he sent a bullet at a gap between two rocks around seventy-five yards from his hiding place.

No, the two men had not gone *loco*. In fact they acted with speed and in complete sanity. As they left their horses, two shots were fired form the places at which they threw their lead. Had they been sitting the horses instead of dropping to the ground, each one of them would have been hit and badly hurt.

Their moves had been timed just right. Having seen certain distant, but alarming movements, both the Kid and Joe expected trouble. They also prepared to deal with it. By singing and acting in such an unconcerned manner, the Kid lulled their waiting attackers' suspicions and led them to believe their presence was undetected. Then when the horse gave its warning—an old Comanche trick which the Kid never regretted having taught to Blackie—they took rapid and effective evasive action. An instant later and lead would have found them; while making their move too soon might have given the waiting assailants time to change their aim.

Following the Kid's second shot, a yell arose from the mesquite. Alerting his aim slightly, he fired again. He heard the dull "whomp!" of a bullet striking something more solid than the mesquite's branches, but less so than rock or earth, followed by a crash and thrashing sound that died off gradually.

Although Barefoot Joe's bullet struck where he aimed it, he heard the vicious scream of a ricochet and doubted if he achieved anything against his attempted killer. Nothing happened, the man between the rocks did not fire again and Joe remained still with the inborn patience of the Indian.

"He get you, Joe?" asked the Kid.

"Missed," the hunter answered. "How about you?"

"Landed on a rock when I lit down. It hurts like hell."

"You *Pehane* never worth a cuss on horses."

"We're all right on the damned things. It's falling off 'em where we have our trouble," drawled the Kid. "Reckon we ought to go take a look?"

Despite the soft-spoken levity, the two men remained alert and their eyes scoured the range ahead of them for any sign of further attackers. While wanting to get to grip with the men who tried to kill them, they knew the value of patience and discretion at such a moment.

"Give 'em just a spell longer," Joe suggested. "They wasn't Injuns and I never saw a white man's could sit this sort of thing out."

Ten minutes dragged by. Ahead of where the two men lay, their horses waited patiently. At last the Kid raised his head, his keen ears detecting certain sounds beyond the rim from which the bullets came.

"One of 'em's pulled out," he said. "Get set!"

With that he launched himself forward from his cover, making a swerving run which took him to the stallion. Going over the horse's seventeen hand high rump like a bullfrog jumping to avoid a raccoon, the Kid landed in the saddle. Immediately the white sprang forward, building its speed up like it had been trained on a quarter-mile racetrack. Riding as if part of the racing horse, the Kid kept his rifle held ready and steered towards the mesquite. Happen one of their attackers ran, it would most likely be Joe's man; or that soggy "whomp!" heard by the Kid after shooting had lied.

Although Joe kept his rifle lined, finger caressing the trigger and eyes searching the area ahead for danger, and the Kid rode ready to make another rapid separation from the horse, nothing happened. Tossing his leg over the saddle horn, the Kid dropped to the ground while Blackie still ran. He lit down with an almost cat-footed agility and plunged into the bushes. For all that he felt sure he did not need it, the Kid held his Winchester ready and moved with caution. He saw the body of a man he recognized lying sprawled on the ground and needed only one quick check to know the precautions had been unnecessary; not that he regretted having taken them. It seemed that his second bullet nicked the man's ear, evoking the yelp of pain which allowed him to correct his aim. How well he corrected showed in that the third bullet caught the man in the center of the chest. In falling, the man had made the thrashing noises as his limbs beat their last frenzied tattoo before death claimed him. It was Plaid, the bulky hard-case who tried to jump Joe the previous day and went through the window for his pains.

Hooves thundered as Joe came tearing by. After covering the Kid, the hunter collected his mount and charged up the slope in hope of seeing the second of their attackers. By the time he topped the rim, however, the fleeing man had disappeared and Joe halted his horse to wait for the Kid.

"It was most likely the other jasper who jumped you in the store," the Kid commented on hearing of Joe's lack of success. "That's his pard lying in the mesquite there."

"Maybe so wanted to get even with us for yesterday," Joe answered. "Other feller not take his hoss."

"We can use it for taking the body into town," the Kid said.

On going to collect the horse, the Kid heard a metallic click in one of the saddlebags. Opening it and inserting his hand, he withdrew an object which brought an angry grunt from Joe's lips.

"That's a trap like the one nearly got you yesterday," the hunter growled.

"Sure is," the Kid agreed. "Maybe those pair wanted more than evens. Looks like they aimed to set up as wolfers."

While there were no game hunting laws in Texas at that time, and wolves ranked as vermin to be exterminated on sight, the ranchers tended to prefer hiring an expert when predators raided their herds. With a master hand like Barefoot Joe in the area, all calls for assistance went to him and less able men would find the going very hard in competition with such expertise as his Comanche upbringing and training gave.

Yet the pickings hardly seemed to warrant a murder attempt without another, deeper motive backing it. That reward offered by Schweitzer, although directed to the Kid, might have provided an inducement and their hatred of Joe given them all the incentive they needed. Nor would folk be likely to question the two if they brought in the body of the man blamed for murdering the well-liked storekeeper. The Kid did not doubt that his own body would have been left hidden on the range, so as to avoid awkward questions, and the killers insist that they never saw him.

"They not do it now," Joe said.

"This one won't, that's for sure," agreed the Kid. "Let's get them into town."

After loading Plaid's body across his saddle, the Kid and Joe continued the interrupted journey. However the Kid changed his mind as he rode. Instead of taking the body in with them, they left it concealed in a hollow a short distance away on the range.

Word ran fast through the town that the Kid had returned with Barefoot Joe and people began to gather on the main street as the two men rode by. Watching everything as always, the Kid noticed that a group of men came from the saloon, and he heard the low, ugly muttering which rose from among them. A growing procession followed the two men and the Kid listened to various comments with growing apprehension. While serving with Dusty Fog as a deputy in Quiet Town, he had seen a lynch mob form and recognized the symptoms in the crowd which trailed along in his wake. Clearly Barefoot Joe also felt uneasy.

"Maybe so I should've done as Solon said and stopped away," he said and dropped his gaze to the rifle in his saddleboot.

"Forget it," ordered the Kid, having persuaded the other to boot the Winchester before they entered town.

"Them not sound friendly."

"Nothing'll happen to you," promised the Kid and hoped he sounded more certain than he felt.

Much to his relief, the Kid saw Blevins step from the store and halt on the porch; although the sight of Schweitzer following on the sheriff's heels did not add to it. For a moment the fat man halted, staring at the two riders as if he could hardly believe his eyes.

"Howdy Kid, Joe," Blevins greeted, throwing a glance at the following crowd. "We'd best go down to the jail house."

"I see you brought him in like you said, Kid," Schweitzer put in.

"Joe didn't need any bringing," the Kid corrected. "When I told him what had happened, he said he'd best come with me."

"He—He's still armed!" the storekeeper yelped. "Take his guns and arrest him, sheriff!"

"There's no need for that!" called a voice from the crowd. "We can soon save the county the cost of a trial and hanging."

Next moment the Kid landed on his feet before the assembled people. He moved with such speed that not one of them had any idea of what he planned until he lit down facing them, his rifle in his hands. Casual and relaxed though he might appear at first glance, none of the watching crowd regarded him in that light. To them he gave the impression of latent, deadly readiness, like a cougar crouched for an attack. His right hand coiled around the small of the rifle's butt, three fingers in the lever ring and the fourth resting on the trigger. No man of the Kid's ability placed his fingers on a weapon's trigger unless he stood ready and prepared to do some shooting.

"Just what's that mean, *hombre?*" asked the Kid, picking out the man he figured to have spoken.

A dull flush came to the man's cheeks at finding himself singled out in such a manner. Like most of the crowd's front rank, he was a man with a truculent air that stemmed either from righteous wrath or liberal dosings with bottled trouble-maker. Whichever it might, he exuded menace.

"We've got a rope right ready and handy and there's a good strong beam in the saloon," he explained, confident of the backing of the crowd.

"And you figure to use 'em?" the Kid inquired.

"That's just what we figure."

Despite his bluff words, the man felt uneasy at being selected as spokesman for the crowd. A loafer of the kind who infested the cattle country towns, the man avoided work as much as possible, joined any crowd which tolerated his kind and was ready to become involved in such fuss as promised a cheap excitement and no risks. Only for once he found himself regarded as a ring-leader. True the bunch who drank in the saloon might be backing him, but they did not have the full support of the rest of the crowd.

Sensing that so far the assembled people were not united in any purpose, the Kid acted fast.

"If that's the way you want it, come ahead," he offered. "All you have to do is pass me."

Gently though he spoke, the Kid found no takers for his offer. None of the crowd moved, for all knew exactly what he meant. It did not take the mental powers of a genius to figure that the Kid stood full ready to back his thrown-down challenge. Nor did anyone present labor, under the illusion that he might be bluffed out. The only way to pass the Kid was by shooting him down.

Of course, it might be argued, he was but one man against a crowd; but each of them possessed only one life. In the hands of a master, the Winchester rifle could spew out lead at better than two shots a second and held fifteen bullets. Given anything like a chance, the Kid would make things mighty unpleasant for those of the crowd closest to him should the need arise.

Other points came to mind once the crowd started thinking. Enough people in town remained uncommitted to make the matter uncertain. Some of them were sure to remain loyal to the sheriff and rally in his aid; enough to make the position of the potential lynch mob anything but a sinecure. Nor did the Ysabel Kid's identity be ignored. Should he go under fighting a mob, his killers would soon come to regret their actions. Cut one member of Ole Devil's floating outfit and the rest bled. As soon as word reached the OD Connected, the floating outfit and the rest of that tough, handy crew were sure to be riding after the man who killed their *amigo*. It would go hard on any and everybody connected with the Kid's death when the vengeance-seeking party arrived.

Sensing the hesitation, Blevins wasted no time in consolidating the Kid's work. Striding forward, the sheriff halted on the edge of the sidewalk. His eyes raked the crowd, only stopping to stare down and quell anyone who attempted to meet his gaze.

"That's it over, boys," Blevins stated. "There'll be no lynching in my town."

Even as he said the word "lynching", Blevins saw a slight change come over the crowd. While they might like to think that they performed an act of simple justice, all knew the exact nature of their behavior; knew it and tried to evade the issue. Put bluntly to them, all realized that they could no longer pretend to be acting in the interest of the law.

"What you fixing to do, sheriff?" called somebody safely at the rear of the crowd.

"What you pay me to do," Blevins answered. "Now let's have this meeting broke off and the street cleared."

Slowly, almost reluctantly it seemed, the crowd began to disperse. Firm and resolute handling ended what might have developed into an ugly incident. Yet the danger had not ended, as Blevins well knew. Turning, he looked at the Kid who slid his Winchester back into the boot.

"Close," the Kid said.

"Real close," agreed Blevins. "Let's go down to the jail."

"You do what I said?"

Before leaving town, the Kid made certain requests which Blevins could understand. The sheriff nodded and replied, "Sure. Schweitzer bitched about it, but I told him that was how it had to be. Shall we take Joe down to the jail?"

"Nope. Let's go inside the store first," the Kid answered and looked around. "Where's Schweitzer?"

"He ducked back when you started facing them yahoos down."

Bounding on to the porch, the Kid darted across it and into the store. He found Schweitzer about to start sweeping up the flour scattered on the floor from the overturned barrel.

"Leave it lie a spell longer, mister," the Kid ordered.

For a moment it seemed that Schweitzer intended to carry on with his proposed cleaning. Then Blevins entered, took one look at the broom and gave out with a deep, annoyed growl.

"Damn it, Mr. Schweitzer," he snapped. "I thought I said for you to leave everything be until you got the word."

"But I thought it wouldn't matter now that you've got the ha—hunter brought in," Schweitzer protested.

"Give us a few minutes, mister," the Kid drawled. "Then you can clean up."

"What's on your mind, Kid?" Blevins inquired.

"Maybe you should have a couple of witnesses in, Tony," the Kid suggested.

Satisfying the request took little effort on the sheriff's part. On going to the door, he found the Wells Fargo agent and his swamper approaching along the sidewalk. Each man carried a shotgun, having gathered them from the sheriff's office before coming to offer their services if needed in quelling the crowd. When Blevins brought the pair into the store, he found that the Kid still was not entirely satisfied.

"Get two of those yahoos who did all the fussing outside to come as well," the dark young Texan requested.

"What's all this about?" demanded Schweitzer indignantly.

"You-all wanted the man who killed your partner, mister," the Kid replied. "So I aim to give him to you."

"I see—Did you have any trouble bringing him in?"

"Nope," lied the Kid. "Should I have had?"

The sheriff entered, followed by two of the crowd, preventing Schweitzer from answering the Kid's question. Clearly surprised at being invited, the two men looked around them and then walked across to examine the tracks in the spilled flour. With that done, they directed their attention to Barefoot Joe and showed interest in his lack of foot-wear.

"All right, Kid," Blevins said. "Is that all your want-ings?"

"I reckon so," the Kid answered.

"What's it all about?" asked Schweitzer, but he no longer spoke in the arrogant, demanding tone.

"Like I said," the Kid told him. "To get the man who killed your partner." He looked at the last pair of men to enter and went on, "That's what we all want, I reckon."

"It sure is," one of them replied.

"And you pair of gents figure that Joe's the one you want?"

"Look at them tracks?" the man answered. "Who else goes barefoot hereabouts?

"They sure are plain," admitted the Kid. "And they were for sure made by a feller without boots or socks."

"Anybody can see that."

"Like you say. The toes show up as clear as day," drawled the Kid. "Walk across the flour there, Joe, will you?"

Watched by the men, Joe obeyed the Kid's request and left behind him clear impressions of his feet in the white surface. With the exception of Schweitzer, the men followed the hunter's movements. Face working nervously and wet with sweat, Schweitzer backed off until he reached the counter. Then he stood silent, his right hand in his jacket's pocket.

"Hey!" yelped one of the independent witnesses, pointing to Joe's footprints. "They're not the same size and look different."

"I could have told you they would be," drawled the Kid calmly. "Fact being I knew from the start Joe hadn't left them."

"How?" Schweitzer said hoarsely.

"Look at the toes. Joe's never worn boots and his toes are spread apart."

"So?" asked the storekeeper.

"The trouble with wearing boots is they squeeze the toes together, just like on the other set. As soon as I saw that, I knew Joe hadn't made them tracks."

"Then who did?" demanded the Wells Fargo agent.

"Somebody who had something to gain from Eli Benjiman's death," the Kid replied. "Who could get in here without busting through the window. And who knew that the jail safe couldn't've been locked 'cause it never is."

"But who was it?" insisted the agent.

"I'd say Mr. Schweitzer," the Kid answered and turned to face the storekeeper. "Why'd you kill your partner, *hombre?*"

"You—You're *loco!*" Schweitzer gasped.

"Then why'd you tell us that his throat'd been cut?"

"I—I saw it through the window."

"All you could see of him was his feet," the Kid pointed out. "Unless you'd been inside here you couldn't've known how he'd been killed."

"He's right at that," the old swamper stated. "Tony fetched me along and let me look through the window afore they moved the body."

"That doesn't prove I killed him!" Schweitzer snarled.

"One of those two jaspers you sent to kill Joe and me told us you did just afore he died," the Kid said.

"They didn't know I'd done it!" screeched Schweitzer and the full import of his words struck him an instant too late to prevent their being uttered.

With a snarl, the storekeeper started to jerk his hand from the pocket and it clearly held a weapon. In his haste, he managed to tangle the Remington's hammer in the lining of the pocket. Panic filled him and he forced down on the gun in an attempt to free it from the clutches of the cloth.

Out came the Kid's great bowie knife and drove towards Schweitzer. Cloth ripped as the razor-sharp blade sliced through Schweitzer's jacket pocket. Forced down by its user's hand, the Derringer came into sight—but it remained just as firmly trapped as Schweitzer's wrist rammed deep into the mouth of the pocket. An instant later Blevins's revolver lined on the storekeeper's fat belly.

"Open your hand and let it fall," the sheriff ordered. "You don't need it at all."

"Damn you!" Schweitzer snarled, glaring at the Kid as he released the Derringer. "If those two fools had killed you this would never have happened."

"Only I wasn't killed," the Kid pointed out. "Why'd you do it?"

"Benjiman was a fool," Schweitzer answered. "He didn't like the way I handled things and aimed to bust up the partnership. I had everything planned—"

"Real good," agreed the Kid. "First off you got in here, knocked Eli down and slit his throat. Then you spilled the flour and walked barefoot through it. That was so everybody'd start blaming Joe. To make sure they did, you went along to the jail and took his skins out of the safe. I'd say you aimed to have him killed afore he could start talking."

"I did. Nobody would worry too much about why the killer of Eli Benjiman came to die," Schweitzer explained. "Those two hard-cases wanted to set up as wolfers and they were set to get the half-breed as he rode in."

"Only I spoiled things a mite," the Kid guessed.

"It'd've worked if you hadn't been here. Or if those two managed to kill you both on the way back to town."

"Waal now," Blevins put in. "I wouldn't say that. Fact being I'd got it all worked out same as the Kid. Only I reckoned he was a mite younger and spryer, so I let him handle things. Let's go down to the jail."

"You get my skins back, sheriff?" Joe asked.

"Unless Schweitzer destroyed 'em."

"Good," the hunter said. "When I sell 'em, I'm going to buy me a pair of boots."

"They squeeze your toes," the Kid pointed out.

"Sure," admitted Joe. "But then I'll make tracks just like everybody else."

PART FOUR

A Tolerable Straight Shooting Gun

Waco did not want to kill Jervis Minshull, but found that the other left him no choice in the matter if he wanted to stay alive himself. When the rich youngster burst out of the Longhorn Saloon in Clinton, he was roaring drunk and had just shot a blackjack dealer after claiming the man cheated.

On hearing the sound of the shot, Waco came along the street at a run. Shooting had long been a cowhand's way of letting off high-spirits, but a single shot almost always meant trouble. However Waco had not drawn his guns when he saw Minshull emerge. Perhaps if Minshull had been sober, he might have recognized his danger and acted in a different manner.

Not that Waco looked particularly dangerous, threatening or aggressive—to Eastern eyes. Six foot in height, blond haired, with a tanned, handsome face that showed intelligence and strength beyond its youthful lines, he wore cowhand clothes which gave off, to Western eyes, the unmistakable signs of a top-hand. Around his waist hung a good quality gunbelt supporting matched staghorn handled Colt Artillery Peacemakers in contoured holsters designed for a real fast draw. That rig told a significant story to a man who knew the range country.

Unfortunately Minshull lacked the necessary knowledge. An education in a number of high-priced private schools and colleges back East—all of which eventually came around to deciding that money could not cover accepting his continued presence—did not include gun-fighting, or other basic essentials needed to survive in frontier Texas. Where, drunk or sober, any native Texan would have taken warning, Minshull saw only a tall youngster wearing the badge of a deputy sheriff pinned to his calfskin vest. With his father's wealth to back him, Minshull had never had need to fear the law in consequence of his actions.

"Hold it, *hombre!*" Waco ordered, "Drop the gun!"

Instead of obeying, Minshull snarled out a curse and fired a shot. As the bullet tore by Waco's head, his right hand dipped in that smoothly effortless-seeming manner which set the master gun fighter apart from the merely good one. Out flowed the off-side Colt, hammer drawn back and trigger depressed, ready for use a bare three-quarters of a second from Minshull's shot. Yet Waco held his fire. He saw the other's condition and prepared to give Minshull a second chance. Again the rich youngster shot, his bullet tearing Waco's Stetson off. Instantly the blond Texan skidded to a halt and cut loose with his Colt. He shot the only way he dared under the circumstances, to kill, for the other started cocking his weapon and clearly meant to try once more. Caught in the head by a .45 bullet, Minshull slammed backwards and fell. He was dead before his body struck the sidewalk.

There had been a time when Waco would not have hesitated in the manner, or thought of giving the other man such an edge as he had by allowing Minshull to take the second shot. Once he would have shot first, relishing the chance of matching his speed against another man's. Those days ended when Dusty Fog risked life and limb to rescue Waco from in front of a stampeding herd of cattle.*

Left an orphan almost from birth, during an Indian attack, Waco—he knew no other name—was raised by a Texas rancher. While always treated kindly and well, he drifted away from his foster home at the age of only thirteen. Even so young he always rode with a gun at his belt and spent almost every cent which came his way on buying ammunition. At sixteen he rode as a member of Clay Allison's wild-onion crew and wore a pair of Army Colts; using them with fast, skilled precision many an older man envied. Such skill while riding as a member of the CA ranch could have easily sent Waco down the paths followed by Wes Hardin, Bill Longley and other fast drawing Texans driven to one killing too many. Instead of becoming a man wanted by the law, Waco fell in with Dusty Fog, joined the OD Connected and rode as a member of the floating outfit.

No longer did Waco ride with a long-sized chip on his shoulder. Taking him under their wings, Dusty Fog, Mark Counter and the Ysabel Kid each contributed to his education. They taught him plenty and he forgot nothing of what he learned. From being a trigger-fast-and-up-from-Texas kid, Waco developed into a useful member of range-land society. In addition to being a highly skilled cow and trail hand, he also possessed considerable ability as a peace officer. He learned his trade under Dusty Fog in Mulrooney and would put the training to good use in later years.†

Being an able lawman brought him to Clinton County, separated from the rest of the floating outfit for the first time on an important chore. The local sheriff, an old friend

* Told in *Trigger Fast*.
† Told in *Arizona Ranger, Sagebrush Sleuth, Waco Rides In*.

of Ole Devil Hardin, sent requesting help. He had to attend a convention called by the State Governor and required an able man to run things. Only Waco had been available, but Ole Devil did not hesitate to send the youngster. On the journey, however, Waco met up with Doc Leroy and between them they handled a serious matter concerning the local banker, a saloonkeeper and a professional killer.† Although Doc intended to join the OD Connected, he could not remain in Clinton and rode off about his business leaving Waco to hold down the town until the sheriff returned. Everything had been fairly peaceful for two days; and then Minshull came, killed a man and paid the price for his misdeed.

"I mind him from the last time he was here," commented one of the inevitable crowd which gathered. "Knowed he'd do something and get his-self killed."

"He sure built up for it inside," another went on.

"That's young Minshull," continued a third, who had not been present in the saloon. "What'll his pappy say about this?"

Which point appeared to be concerning and worrying a number of people. Cyrus Minshull was a rich Eastern financier, one of the many who turned to Texas in their search for further profitable speculation. A hard-headed business man who bordered on the unscrupulous in his dealings, he doted upon his only child and had always used his wealth or social position to shield a thoroughly spoilt, selfish youngster from the consequences of a variety of misdeeds. Certainly Minshull senior would never concede that Waco acted in the only manner possible.

After arranging for the two bodies to be taken to the undertaker's premises, Waco settled down to the business

† Told in *The Hard Riders*, Part 5, The Hired Butcher.

of learning why Minshull killed a man. What he discovered softened his feelings at having to shoot the young man. However he knew that the affair had not yet ended.

Proof of that came when he entered the sheriff's office and found three men waiting; influential citizens not entirely disinterested in retaining Cyrus Minshull's goodwill. Although Waco could guess what brought the trio, he waited for them to open the conversation.

"We admit that you acted in self-defense, deputy," started Duprez, acting as manager of the bank while its tangled affairs were settled. "But it may be better for all concerned if you turn in your badge and leave town."

"Will it?" Waco asked mildly.

"Yes. Of course we will pay you in fu—"

"Mister," the youngster interrupted. "I came here to run the law for a good friend of my boss and until he comes back to say he doesn't need me any more I'm staying on to do it."

"We don't want to force you to go—" squawked the second man, Logan, thinking of how Minshull's financial backing would improve the chances of his meat-packing business.

"That's *bueno*," Waco drawled. "'Cause I don't force easy."

Watching the men, Waco knew where the chief danger lay. The third member of the deputation was a different kind of man from his companions. Rich and influential as they were, there the resemblance ended. Logan and Duprez would talk, but nothing more. Not so Eben Firwood. Owner of a successful freighting business, he grew rich through hard work. Freighting did not call for mild-natured men with meek ways and he did not aim to see the chance of gaining plenty of business flip through his blunt, powerful fingers.

"Listen, boy," he began.

"There're only three men who can call me 'boy', mister," Waco told him.

Tough though Firwood might be, he found himself growing uneasy in front of the young Texan's cold blue eyes. Maybe he could use his hard fists to enforce his will, but to do that he had to reach Waco. There would be less than a second to do so, for that was all the time the blond youngster needed to draw and shoot.

At Firwood's side, Duprez exchanged worried glances with Logan. Being more diplomatic than the freighter, and remembering that Waco possessed some mighty influential backing, they wanted the affair smoothing over.

"You know how delicate the situation is in town, deputy," Duprez said. "It was your efforts which brought to light the state of the bank."

"Sure," agreed Waco.

"Then you must understand that Mr. Minshull's backing could make all the difference to us."

"So?"

"So you killed his son!" shouted Firwood. "He's not going to be happy about that."

"How about the dealer's wife and kids?" Waco asked. "Reckon they'll be happy about losing him?"

"He was cheat—" Firwood started.

"Don't try that with me!" Waco barked. "I've watched every game in town and that one's the straightest of them all. The dealer never passed a wrong card. With the edge the house has at blackjack, he doesn't need to."

"Are you calling me a liar?" demanded Firwood.

Waco's chair slid back and he rose, standing tense and watchful. "Now me," he said. "I'd reckon that's up to you to decide."

In Texas the word "liar" could only be accepted in one

way. Knowing that, Firwood once more found himself facing the unpalatable fact of Waco's proven ability in the *pistolero* arts. Few men in town dare to stand up to the burly freighter. The absent sheriff had been one; and that tall blond youngster from the Rio Hondo was another.

"All right," Firwood said. "No hard feelings."

With that he smiled in a disarming manner and raised his right arm. Apparently satisfied, Waco relaxed and accepted the offered hand. Instantly the freighter clamped hold and gave a jerk designed to haul Waco into reach of his bunched left fist. It was a neatly-done move and one which frequently met with success.

Only it went wrong.

Waco had not failed to notice that the placating smile did not reach Firwood's eyes. Nor did he regard the freighter as being a man likely to give up a desired intention so easily. Ready for anything, Waco gave the appearance of going along with Firwood's gesture of goodwill up to a point. After that point Waco steered his own mighty effective path.

On feeling the start of Firwood's pull, Waco threw his weight forward and advanced faster than the man expected. Out shot the youngster's right hand, knotted into a fist and powered by hard muscles, to sink into Firwood's belly. In the days when he drove his own wagon and handled a six-horse team, Firwood had been as tough as any of the bull-whip breed. Recently he spent his time behind a desk, lived well and dined expansively. Such habits did not tend to make for a solid, muscle-guarded belly and Firwood could not take punishment down there. An explosive grunt left him as the air drove from his lungs. He took a pace to the rear, doubling over in an attempt to lessen the pain which knotted his injured stomach.

Throwing up his now-free right hand, Waco smashed its knuckles full under Firwood's jaw. The freighter straightened out once more, shot backwards and crashed into the wall. For a moment he hung there on buckling legs, then shook his head and let out a snarl as he dropped his hand to where he once would have worn a gun.

"Hold it!" Waco barked, right hand dipping and producing its Colt as realization caused Firwood to move forward. "I'll cut your legs from under you if you make a move."

The warning and sight of the gun brought Firwood to a halt. Already he had pushed the affair beyond any bounds of safety and might count himself fortunate to still be alive. Many a man, especially one who took the time to acquire such deadly speed with a gun, would not have hesitated after the treacherous attack. Any further attempts at troublemaking on Firwood's part could easily prove fatal.

"Stop this right now!" yelped Duprez, looking as nervous as a mother hen spooked by a chicken hawk. "You had no right to assault Mr. Firwood!"

"I could throw him in jail for attempting to assault a duly sworn officer of the law," Waco replied. "Which same I'm right likely to do—"

"You don't appear to realize how serious the situation is!" wailed Logan.

"A man's been killed. A woman left a widow and kids fatherless," Waco answered. "Mister, to me, that's damned serious."

"But what can we tell Mr. Minshull?" Logan asked.

"You could tell him the truth," Waco suggested. "Make it as easy as you can, but anyways you look at it, his son got stunk-up drunk, cried cheat when he lost in a straight game and shot down an unarmed man."

"Is that what you say happened?" asked a voice from the door.

Turning. Waco looked at the tall man who entered. Grief

lined the man's hard face, but did not soften it any. He wore expensive, if sober, clothes of the latest Eastern cut and—this Waco noticed first—did not appear to be armed.

"M—Mr. Minshull!" Duprez gasped, confirming Waco's conclusions as to the newcomer's identity.

"We—" Logan started to speak, but trailed off as he could not decide what to say to the grieving father. "Is there anything we can do, Mr. Minshull?"

"I want to speak with this young man alone," Minshull replied curtly.

"He's not a regular deputy," Firwood growled, fingers touching his throbbing jaw and hate in his eyes.

"Leave me with him!" Minshull snapped.

It was a command and the three men, each wealthy by Western standards and important in the community, slunk out of the room like slaves dismissed by their master. Minshull watched them go, then turned and approached the desk. All the time as he drew closer, the financier kept his eyes on Waco's face and seemed to be trying to read everything he could from it. For his part Waco studied Minshull with the same interest. A powerful man, arrogant—as shown by his curt dismissal of Logan, Duprez and Firwood—and shrewd. Genuine grief showed on his face, but under it lay something Waco could not quite catch.

"You were the one," Minshull said, sitting down at the desk.

"Yes," the youngster admitted.

"Tell me about it."

"You won't like what you're going to hear."

"I know my son, he was far from perfect, young man," the financier growled. "Why did you kill him?"

"To stop him killing me," Waco replied.

"Commendable to your way of thinking. But why did he try to kill you?"

Waco did not hesitate. Already he had summed up Minshull's character. There sat a man with whom it would never pay to show weakness or hesitation. In Minshull's eyes, any man who vacillated or failed to stand up to him was a weakling deserving of neither consideration nor respect.

"Your son had been drinnking heavy, took to playing blackjack and got mean when he lost," the youngster said, his voice cold and even, eyes never leaving Minshull's unwinking face. "He allowed he'd been cheated, pulled a gun and shot the dealer."

"And had he been cheated?"

"Not that I could find sign of."

"Were you present in the game?"

"No. But I've been around town long enough to know it was straight. I've watched it without letting the house know and never seen a wrong move made."

"Would you know if there had been?" Minshull asked.

"I know a mite about crooked gambling tricks," Waco answered.

"Such knowledge isn't easy to come by," Minshull commented.

"The man who taught me was a straight gambler. He'd learned so that he knew when other folks tried to cheat him."

"And how would you say one can cheat at blackjack?"

"That's just about the easiest game to cheat at. You play so fast and have your eyes on your own cards most of the time. Then each player starts with only two cards, which makes it easier for the cheat to rig the deck, or remember who holds what and know how to handle them."

"In what way would he handle them?"

"They're a whole slew of ways. Marked cards, so he knows who holds what and can tell the value of the next card to be dealt, is one of the easiest ways happen the dealer can fetch them off the bottom or toss out the second card from the top."

"Is that easy?" Minshull inquired, studying Waco all the time.

"Nope. If the dealer can't do it, he has a feller sat at his right ready to buy off a card that might help the other players."

"And if he doesn't use marked cards?"

"Then he 'peeks'," Waco replied. "Looks at the next card to be dealt."

"How?"

"There's plenty of ways. He can heave a small mirror built into a ring or the bowl of a pipe, or even an extra shiny coin, lying in front of him. Just slides the card forward a mite and reads its value in the reflection. Or he can distract the players for just long enough to bend up the card a mite and see what it is. That's the way most crooked dealers work."

Interest warred with the grief on Minshull's face and he asked. "What about arranging the order of the cards, so they will be favorable to the dealer?"

"'Rigging'?" Waco drawled. "That's done. It means either getting a new deck specially rigged each time, or that the dealer can riffle-stack the cards. Set them up how he wants them in the shuffle before the game."

"Would that be possible?" demanded Minshull.

Reaching into the desk's drawer, Waco removed a deck of cards used to pass the time when things were slack around the office. Normally he would not have shown his ability, but felt doing so might do something to ease Minshull's sense of loss; or make the man forget it for a short time. With the deft skill learned from Frank Derringer in Mulrooney and practiced at every opportunity, Waco showed Minshull much that crooked gamblers would have preferred not to be known outside their own circle. First Waco demonstrated the comparatively easy "overhand stack", working required cards from the bottom of the deck into advantageous positions. Then he showed how to achieve the same end by the more difficult "riffle stack". When Minshull pointed out that the cards must be cut before the deal, Waco showed him how to nullify the cut and return the two parts to their original positions. Then the youngster dealt hands to show how peeking, backed by dealing the bottom, or second from the top, card paid off. All in all it was a masterful display and Minshull sat watching every move with interest.

"You certainly have the ability to detect cheating if there was any," the financier declared, after Waco concluded the display by explaining about the more common ways of marking cards and how to detect the hidden symbols.

"I had me a real good teacher," Waco replied.

"In more ways than one. How old are you?"

"Coming up nineteen."

"Nineteen," Minshull sighed. "My son was twenty and— You are young to be holding such a responsible position. Yet you have done real well as deputy sheriff from all I hear."

"Like I said, I had real good teachers."

"Unfortunately good teachers aren't all it takes," Minshull said sadly. "The willingness to learn must be there too."

"Likely," Waco answered. "I've never thought much on it."

"Tell me a little about yourself, young man," Minshull requested.

"There's not much to tell. I work for the OD Connected

and came along here when the sheriff wrote my boss to ask for help."

"You gave it very well, by all accounts. It was you who discovered that the bank was in a bad way and caught the banker out, wasn't it?"

"I had some help."

"It took shrewd thought and ability," Minshull said, ignoring Waco's comment. "Few youngsters your age would have been able to do it."

"I was just lucky," Waco drawled.

"Luck is only another name for ability in many cases, young man. Are you staying here for long?"

"Until the sheriff comes back from Austin."

"And then?"

"I'll be headed home to the OD Connected. There'll likely be more work for me to do," Waco replied, then he scooped up the cards and dropped them into the drawer. "There's no way I can apologize for your son's death, Mr. Minshull. But if I hadn't shot him, he'd've killed me."

"You did your duty, young man," Minshull answered and rose. "Can I make the arrangements for my son's burial?"

"Sure. If you go to the undertaker's place, he'll see to it. There'll be a coroner's inquiry though."

"When?"

"In a couple of days, I reckon," Waco answered. "I'll have to tell what I found out happened."

"Of course," agreed Minshull, something flickering across his face. "There's no way you could be induced to—shall we say—"

"Make your son look better," Waco suggested.

"To make it appear that he was not a vicious, drunken fool," Minshull growled. "You'd find that I'd not be ungrateful."

"I'm putting this down to grief, mister," Waco said coldly.

"But come what may, when I step in front of the coroner, I'll tell just what happened. And you'd best say no more about it."

Since attaining his present position of wealth and importance, few men dared to stand up to Cyrus Minshull. A mixture of admiration and anger passed across his face and he came to his feet.

"You'll do your duty, young man, as you did it outside the saloon," the financier remarked, standing for a moment looking at Waco. Then abruptly he turned and walked from the office.

Three worried-looking men waited on the sidewalk and gathered around Minshull as he came into sight.

"Is everything all right, Mr. Minshull?" asked Duprez.

"With my son killed in the street like a drunken cowboy?" Minshull snorted.

"We're all deeply sorry about that." Logan assured him. "You know why he was killed?"

"The deputy told me it was because Jervis shot at him while coming from the saloon after falsely accusing and killing a man over a card game."

"The deputy could have been mistaken about the accusation being false," Duprez suggested. "I think he was wrong."

"You believe the dealer cheated?"

"We all do, Mr. Minshull," Duprez replied and the other two muttered their agreement.

"I don't," Minshull stated firmly.

The statement stopped the men in their tracks and they stared at him as if unable to believe their ears. A cold, calculating glint came into Minshull's eyes as he studied the three men who depended so much upon receiving his financial aid.

"My son was a liar, drunkard and trouble-causer," he

continued calmly. "I have known it for years—but I've no wish to have that knowledge made public."

"I don't follow you," Duprez said, putting all the trio's mystification into words.

"It's quite simple. You three need my financial backing. I'm ready to give it to you—"

"After we've done what?" growled Firwood.

"After the coroner's inquest, which will learn that my son was being cheated and shot in self defense."

"But you said—" began Logan.

"I know what I said," admitted Minshull. "And I'm telling you now. Not a thin dime will come your way unless the coroner finds as I want."

With that he walked away, crossing the street and making his way to the hotel. None of the trio moved for a long time, then Firwood—always a man of action—let out an angry snort. The sound jolted his companions out of their amazement and Duprez raised an indignant wail.

"Did you ever see such a cold-blooded—"

"Point being Duprez," Firwood interrupted. "How're we going to fix things for him. Doc Blakeney's coroner and he'll find on the way the evidence goes no matter what we say to him."

"There wouldn't be a handful of people in the saloon when it happened," Logan said. "We might be able to persuade them to testify our way."

"You mean have them say the dealer was cheating?" Duprez gasped.

"Just that," Firwood agreed. "Hell, he's dead now so it can't hurt him."

"No, there's that," admitted Duprez. "I think that we might be able to get everybody in the saloon and make them see reason."

"Let's go and see," ordered Firwood.

The visit to the saloon might have proved successful but for one thing. Only a few customers had been present, townsmen with a stake in keeping Minshull contented, and pressure could have been brought to bear upon the employees. As the saloon's owner owed the bank some money, his cooperation was assured. He brought up a snag to the whole business of faking the evidence by mentioning that Waco had already made a thorough examination of the game and declared it to be fair.

"Who'll believe a kid like that?" demanded Duprez as he left the saloon with his companions.

"That kid was smart enough to uncover the games that Nodern and Hancox had been playing at the bank," Firwood answered. "Blakeney'll listen when he gives evidence and believe him."

"But Morgan could produce a deck of marked cards—" started Logan.

"I suggested that," Firwood told him, remembering the saloonkeeper's vigorous protests when having the suggestion put to him. "He claims that the deputy'd decide he was being called a liar. And Morgan wouldn't chance that."

"Couldn't we approach the deputy?" Duprez asked. "Offer him money—"

"He'd ram it down your throat," Firwood warned. "And don't say everybody has a price. You couldn't bribe that kid with more money than you'll ever have. No, we have to make sure that he doesn't give evidence at the inquest."

"How?" asked Logan.

"There's only one way to do it," stated Firwood grimly. "Kill him."

"K—Kill him!" squawked Logan, staring at the freighter and seeing visions of himself being allocated the task.

"If you gentlemen wish to discuss killing somebody, I'd

suggest a lower tone of voice and less public place," said a voice from behind the trio.

While talking, they had come to a halt on what they imagined to be a deserted strip of the sidewalk. Swinging around, all three stared at the speaker whose silent approach brought him close enough to overhear their words. He proved to be a small sharp-featured man dressed in town clothes; a nondescript individual who they might easily have overlooked as of no importance had it not been for his comments on the subject under discussion.

"What the hell's your game, sneaking up and listening to private conversations?" snapped Duprez in the tone he reserved for unimportant people. However he found the little man's eyes disturbing, cold and in some way menacing.

After one quick glance in the banker's direction, the small man turned his attention to Firwood.

"It's lucky that you're hiring an expert to do your killing," he told the freighter. "My name's Ross. Your clerk pointed you out to me when I asked for you at the office and I came straight along."

"So you're Ross," Firwood breathed. "I sent for you a fair time back."

"And I'd other clients needing me," the small man answered. "It seems that you still need my services."

"I thought we might need help with Nodern and Hancox," Firwood told his companions. "So I sent for Ross here. Only that deputy dealt with them before he came. You nearly had a wasted journey, Mr. Ross."

"I'd've been paid for it," Ross replied with complete confidence. "Now, I don't mince words. Who do you want killed?"

"Come eighter from Decatur. Baby wants a new pair of shoes!"

Two dice bounced across the ground and landed almost at Waco's feet as he approached the rear of the livery barn on his way to tend to his horse. Several Negroes standing or kneeling in a rough half circle looked up at him. Bending, Waco took up the dice, meaning to return them to the field of play.

"We gennelmen is only indulging in a game of skill, sheriff," stated a tall, gangling beanpole with a cheery face, who Waco recognized as working in the livery barn.

Murmurs of agreement came from all but one of the players. The latter was big, bulky and wore a flashy suit of Eastern cut. From his position, he had been shooting the dice and requesting assistance to throw an eight point. Looking up, he scowled at Waco.

"Gambling ain't illegal, ofay," he said. "Just you toss them dice down here and leave law-abiding folks to their doings."

Up to that point Waco had been on the verge of returning the dice. However, a Negro only used the word "ofay" to a white man as an insult and Waco did not take insults mildly. Clearly the other players did not share the speaker's views.

"There ain't no call for that kind of talk, Herbert," stated the beanpole. "You slung the dice over there and the sheriff done nothing but picked 'em up to hand back."

For a moment the burly man scowled, then gave a shrug. "All right. No offense meant, white boy."

Which came mighty close to an apology, especially as he spoke with the accent of a Negro from well north of the Mason-Dixie line and so did not know the dangers of acting tough with an armed man. Not wanting trouble with the colored element of the town. Waco nodded his agreement.

"None took," he said and opened his hand.

Just as he was about to toss the dice back, Waco saw a

glint of relief come to Herbert's face. Something in the way the man stared at his hand aroused his suspicions and he turned the dice over with a forefinger.

"Just toss them galloping dominoes back here, white boy," ordered Herbert.

"A game of skill, huh," Waco said quietly.

"You hand 'em over here, right quick!" Herbert spat out.

"There wouldn't be something wrong wid them cubes, now would there, sah?" asked the beanpole.

"That depends," Waco replied.

"On what, sah?"

"On how many twos, threes and sixes there should be on each dice."

"You give 'em here!" bellowed Herbert, lunging up from the ground and advancing on Waco with a rush.

Despite the speed of the man's attack, Waco could see that he did not come blindly. As he drew near, Herbert launched a punch straight at the Texan's head. The attack came fast and deadly and the Negro handled himself like he had more than a little experience of fist-fighting. There were many lawmen—not all of whom fought for or supported the Confederacy during the Civil War—who would have immediately used a .45 bullet to halt a black man. Waco had learned the peace officer's trade from a man who believed that the gun must only be used as a last resort when faced with an unarmed assailant. So he prepared to deal with the man in a manner learned from Dusty Fog.

As the fist lashed at his head, Waco brought up his own tight hand in a snappy chopping move which deflected the assailant's arm to the left. From there Waco's hand passed under the man's arm and across to grasp the shoulder of his jacket. As he moved forward, allowing the Negro to pass him under the impetus of the averted blow, Waco brought up his left hand to catch Herbert's right elbow from below.

Then Waco swung his right leg across to strike the back of Herbert's calf and at the same time thrust back with his right arm. The combination of movements came so swift and unexpected that the man could do nothing to counter it. His feet left the ground and he landed hard upon his back.

When the trouble started, the remaining players in the dice game rose and glided away with the exception of the tall thin man. Instead of following his companions, he stood and watched with some surprise as Waco elected to use hands and not a gun against Herbert.

Usually Waco would have followed the throw up by bending the trapped arm against its elbow joint over his leg, or twisted it around behind the man's back. Figuring that the other would have learned his lesson, the youngster stepped clear. In falling two more pair of dice had jolted from the pockets of Herbert's fancy vest and Waco wished to examine them. So, apparently, did the lean man for he walked forward.

"I don't know how you done it, sah," he said amiably. "But you surely did. Now I'd surely admire to look at them dices."

"They're there," Waco answered, nodding to the pair he dropped when preparing to handle Herbert's attack.

Scooping up the dice, the local man turned them between his fingers and found them to be unusual, although he fully understood their purpose. A normal dice is numbered from one through to six on its faces, the sum of each pair of opposite faces adding to seven. On the pair held the two, three and sixes each had their numbers duplicated on the opposite side. As it was impossible for any player to see more than three faces without taking up the dice and turning them between the fingers, the deception went unnoticed during the play of the game. Such dice gave the shooter an unbeatable advantage.

When the shooter at craps threw a point number, he must repeat it before rolling a seven. Using dice such as the slim Negro examined, Herbert could not in any way make the losing seven and might continue to roll in the assurance that sooner or later he must produce his required eight.

Picking up the other four dice, Waco found, as he expected, that they covered those aspects of the game not met by the first pair. Two of them proved to be honest and would be used when other than Herbert acted as the shooter. On his turn to shoot coming around, Herbert either switched one of the dishonest pairs in or made the first throw with the straight dice and decided on what course to follow when he saw the number he achieved. The final pair of dice had one with only a two, four and six on it, while the other bore only a one, three and five; a combination guaranteeing more than its share of sevens.

So engrossed did Waco become, examining the dice and wondering which method their owner used when making a switch of pairs, that he took his attention from the bulky man. Thrusting himself upright, Herbert threw a punch which caught Waco under the jaw and sent him crashing backwards. The blow dazed the young Texan, but his horseman's instinct caused him to break the worst of his fall. From striking Waco, Herbert's hand dipped under his jacket and emerged with a cut-throat razor which he flicked open in a professional manner.

"Hey now, you-all stop that!" yelled the slim Negro, knowing what might easily happen to the colored population of Clinton should Waco be killed by Herbert.

"You wanting it 'stead of him, Sammy?" Herbert spat and swung towards the other man.

Showing an agility which told he understood the use of a razor, Sammy avoided the first raking slash and in doing so gave Waco a much-needed respite. Waco shook his head to clear it and looked up in time to see Herbert drive across another slash in Sammy's direction. Coming to his feet fast, Waco drew his right hand Colt, fired to make the luckiest shot of his life.

"Wha—!" Herbert squalled as the blade of his razor shattered under the impact of the bullet; although it must be said that Waco did not aim for such a spectacular effect.

Gliding forward, Waco whipped his Colt's barrel across Herbert's jaw and dropped him to the ground. Before he could recover, Waco drew the handcuffs from his hip pocket to secure the powerful black wrists.

"Now that was real fancy shooting, sah," Sammy said admiringly.

"It would've been happen I'd tried it," grinned Waco. "Thanks, you drew him off me."

"Waal, I has to clean up around here and sure hates moving blood. And you for sure saved me right back. Fact is you has saved my life and fambly fortune today."

"Talking about that last," Waco said, touching his jaw and wincing. "You'd best gather up the money on the floor there and share it among the other players while I take this festive jasper off to jail."

"You could leave him with us," Sammy suggested innocently. "We gone got us a preacher down here who preaches a mighty purty sermon on the evils of using crooked dice."

"I bet you have," Waco replied. "Only I'm like you, I have to clean up—"

"You is way past me right now."

"I have to do it 'round town and I hate having to clean up bodies."

"The point is took," stated Sammy.

Watching Waco escort the handcuffed and dazed Herbert away in the direction of the jail, Sammy nodded approvingly. Many peace officers would not have shown such leniency and several Sammy had met in his travels around Texas would have taken the stakes of the game instead of leaving them to be shared among the honest players. Whistling cheerily, the lean man gathered the money and entered the barn.

After Waco had jailed Herbert, he returned to the front office and began to fill in the log on the desk. While doing so, he heard the door open and saw that Minshull stood just inside.

"I heard you have my servant here, deputy," the financier said.

"You mean the man I brought in?"

"Yes. What is he to be charged with?"

"That depends on him."

"What did he do?" Minshull snapped.

"I caught him using 'missouts' in a dice game."

"Missouts?" said Minshull.

"These," Waco answered and waved a hand to the three sets of dice on the desk. "He had a straight set, 'missouts' that can't throw a seven and 'hits' that can. So I brought him in."

Knowing something of his servant's temper, Minshull looked hard at the Texan. From the dull bruise on Waco's jaw, Herbert had resisted and Minshull was aware of the man's ability as a fist-fighter.

"Is he injured?" demanded the financier.

"Got a sore jaw is all. I laid a pistol barrel across it to stop him using a razor on one of the other players. Then I figured I'd best put him in jail until things cooled down."

"I can promise you he'll make no more trouble."

"It's not him I'm worried about," Waco told the financier. "The rest of the players'll likely be riled about him. Which same's the main reason why I brought him in."

"Herbert can take care of himself," Minshull remarked.

"Likely," Waco drawled. "Only I'm paid to keep the peace and that includes among the black folks as well as the whites."

Once more the financier found himself admiring the calm, competent way in which Waco acted and comparing it with the behavior of his dead son. There were few men who could have brought Herbert in single-handed and without seriously injuring the man. Yet that tall youngster did so.

"What will happen to him?" Minshull asked.

"Comes morning he'll go afore the judge, have a fine slapped on him and be turned loose."

"Can't I pay the fine now?"

"That depends on the judge," Waco replied. "If you like, we'll walk along to his office and see what he says."

The evening breeze blew coolly along Clinton's main street as Waco and Minshull left the sheriff's office and watched Herbert slouch in the direction of the hotel. As Waco expected, the local judge raised no objections to freeing Minshull's servant on the payment of a fine and receiving the financier's assurance that the Negro would keep away from any of the other players in the game.

"Reckon he'll do it?" Waco asked.

"Herbert knows better than disobey me," Minshull assured him.

Before the youngster could learn why the financier felt so sure of Herbert's obedience, he heard a shot followed by a second. They came spaced evenly apart, not in the manner of a wild volley such as a celebrating cowhand might turn loose.

"I'd best take a look," Waco stated.

"Mind if I come along?" asked Minshull.

"Come ahead," the youngster invited. "But if there's trouble keep well back."

On locating the source of the shooting, Minshull did not need to keep back. Beyond the town a group of local businessmen gathered to watch a tall, lean dude firing a revolver at a distant target.

"Howdy, deputy," greeted Svenson, owner of the town's largest hardware store. "Reckon we should have told you about this. Mr. Tomkins here's a gun salesman and brought us out to see how well this new Smith & Wesson shoots."

While Waco had correctly identified the maker of the revolver, he saw on closer inspection it differed in certain minor details from the old 1869 Army Model or the Russian Model which one usually saw. With its eight inch barrel, it looked long and lean in comparison to the Colt Peacemaker and appeared to have the typical saw-handle butt of the Smith & Wesson company.

"It's the Schofield Model, deputy," Tomkins said. He was a tall man dressed in a check suit, derby hat and with a lean face with a neatly trimmed beard. ".45 Center-fire caliber, two hundred and eighteen grain, round-nosed, outside lubricated bullet. It's an even more accurate round than our old .44 Russian."

"It sure is," enthused one of the onlookers. "He's been hitting that there target real regular."

Which Waco conceded to be real good shooting, the target hanging on a tree a good seventy-five yards away. Breaking open the revolver, Tomkins ejected its empty cases and slid six more bullets into the chambers. He closed the action, raised the revolver in the classic dueling-target stance and fired once more. At the side of the tree, Svenson's son tapped the center of the twenty-six inch white paper target to show where the bullet struck.

"Another hit," whooped Svenson. "Can you equal that for shooting, Waco?"

"Happen I want to hit anything that far off, I'd use a rifle," Waco replied.

"You wouldn't want to match shots for side bets then, deputy?" asked Tomkins.

"Not unless you'd let me use the rifle."

"I did hear you reckon on being something of a gun artist."

"Whoever told you that got me mixed up with Wyatt Earp."

A chuckle ran through the crowd at Waco's reply. While few of its members had been up trail to Dodge, the Texas newspapers gave them a fairly accurate idea of the truth and fictions circulating about the Kansas peace officer. Many highly colored stories about Earp's shooting skill made the rounds, but few Texans believed them to be true.

"Then you don't aim to show us how good you are, deputy?" asked Firwood, in the crowd with his two companions.

"Nope," answered Waco.

"Maybe this gent's a whole lot better than you," the freighter continued.

"I'd say that's tolerable likely," Waco drawled. "Otherwise he wouldn't've been sent to Texas to show off the new Smith & Wesson."

"Come on, deputy," Duprez said. "Show us how you dropped that hired butcher."

"That'll be easy," Waco replied. "I didn't drop him, it was Doc Leroy and they stood a whole heap closer together than seventy-five yards."

"Looks like the deputy likes his shooting easy," Tomkins remarked.

Although the man spoke lightly, his voice held the hint

of a mocking sneer. Waco did not entirely care for the attitude but held himself in check. Most likely Tomkins hoped to rile him into a shooting match designed to prove the superiority of the Smith & Wesson Schofield revolver over the Peacemaker and Waco wanted no part in such an affair. Having been reared on a Colt and owing his life to the products of Colonel Sam's Hartford factory, Waco saw no reason to show the Peacemaker's limitations—he admitted that it had a few—to help boost the sales of another company's weapon.

"Give me the choice and I'd as soon not have shooting at all," he said and turned to walk away.

"It looks like our fast-gun deputy's not so hot after all," Firwood announced in a carrying tone.

"Maybe not," Svenson sniffed. "But I'd sure as hell not want him shooting at me."

"From what I've just seen, I'd rather have him than Mr. Tomkins here throwing lead my way," Firwood declared. "Show us some more of what that new gun can do, friend. I may buy one myself."

Waco continued to walk, ignoring the comments. At his side Minshull shot him an appraising glance. Instead of joining the businessmen, Minshull had turned and accompanied the young Texan. A few eyes followed their departure, but swung back to watch Tomkins once more.

"Why didn't you take up the challenge?" Minshull asked.

"Hell, I can't equal that kind of shooting," Waco answered frankly. "Like I said, at seventy-five yards, happen I've the chance, I'd use a rifle."

"Would it have hurt to have tried?"

"It could have," Waco said. "Any lawman who shows he can use a gun's likely to get hot-heads wanting to try him out. If he's real good, they think long and hard about it afore trying. Happen I'd gone up against that feller and got licked, which I would, word'd've got around. Then some damn fool kid starts thinking, 'He can't be so good, way that city feller beat him.' Next thing I know, the kid's stood in front of me and telling me to reach for my gun."

"The same thing could still happen through your refusal to try."

"Maybe," admitted Waco. "But the same fool kid won't know for sure that I couldn't've licked that salesman had I tried."

"And, of course, it wouldn't do your self-confidence any good to face the man and be beaten," Minshull remarked.

"I never thought of that," Waco replied. "Most likely nobody'll mention it now nothing happened, but they for sure would have happen I'd stacked up against Tomkins and got licked."

Again Waco found the financier to be studying him with that curious mixture of annoyance and admiration. However his refusal to match skill against Tomkins received no more discussion and they parted at the hotel. Going to the Longhorn Saloon, Waco ate a meal and then gave thought to making the rounds of the town.

Towards ten o'clock that evening Waco started his rounds. While he expected no trouble, he stayed alert and strolled along with eyes darting glances about him. A low hiss drew his attention to a dark alley between two closed business premises and he could make out a dark shape standing against the right side wall.

"Come on out here!" Waco ordered, ready to take any action necessary in the event of attack.

"I'd as soon stay in here, sheriff," replied a familiar voice. "It's Sammy from the livery barn and I's something to tell you-all."

"What's wrong, Sammy?" Waco asked, joining the gangling man in the alley.

"Somebody's fixing to kill you-all, sah. I heard 'em talking about it down to the livery barn."

"Who was it?"

"I dunno. See, after the game bust up, I figured to catch me some sleep that I missed last night and went into an empty stall. Waal, I'd just dropped off when two fellers come in wid hosses. I was just fixing to git up and help when there's another one walk in. He says that they's going to kill the deputy."

"And you didn't see them?"

"I didn't try, and that's for true," Sammy stated. "I figures that folks talking that a-ways wouldn't take kind to finding that a colored gennelman done accidently heard 'em."

"Can't say I blame you," Waco admitted. "How long ago was this?"

"Maybe half an hour after we done had that unpleasantness."

Which made it a fair time back. Long enough for his would-be killers to have scattered off into town. All he could do was keep a careful watch on any strangers, no easy task in a town which drew much trade from travelers.

After thanking the man for the warning, Waco continued his rounds. While walking, he gave thought to the forthcoming attempt on his life. Finding the killers might not be easy for they had had time to scatter and might be anywhere in town. Three strangers, as long as they kept separated until making their move, would attract no attention around town.

A further line of thought opened up. Who in Clinton wanted Waco dead bad enough to hire it done?

Two obvious suspects sprang to mind. Minshull undoubtedly had cause to hate Waco; but so did friends of Nodern and Hancox. It had been decided to hold the banker and gambler in Jeffville until their trial, which did not mean they could be discounted as a factor. Maybe Nodern hired killers to remove one of the lawmen responsible for his arrest and who would be giving evidence at his trial. Off hand Waco could not think of any other person who wanted him dead.

Following the training given to him by Dusty Fog, Waco tried to guess when the killers aimed to strike. He almost welcomed shouts coming from the Longhorn and the sight of a waiter leaping into the street. Given a chance of action, he put aside thoughts and sprang forward.

"Fight, deputy," the waiter told him.

On entering the saloon. Waco found two men struggling together. Both appeared to be dudes, which did not make the fight even as there was a big difference in their sizes. Waco moved forward, catching the collar of the bigger man and heaving him away from the small, nondescript, inoffensive jasper who flailed inexpertly with wild fists.

"Finish it off, gents!" Waco barked.

Instead of obeying, the big dude lunged forward and Waco back-handed him hard. As he rocked back on his heels, the man started to reach under his jacket. An instant later he looked into the bore of the youngster's right hand Colt and froze.

"That's better," Waco said. "What's the fuss?"

"This pair were playing poker peaceable enough and all of a sudden the lil feller yells he's been cheated," the waiter who had attracted Waco's attention explained. "Bouncers aren't in tonight, so I come looking for you."

"How about it, mister?" Waco asked the smaller man.

"He's been cheating. Nobody could be that lucky."

"Damned fool!" spat the big dude, a surly young man in a cheap suit.

"You just stand there while I take a look," ordered Waco.

Holstering his Colt, the youngster gathered up the cards and formed them into a deck. Gripping it firmly in his left hand, Waco riffled the upper edges of the cards with his right thumb and watched their surfaces. At first the design remained constant, then it varied. Halting his movement, Waco thumbed back through the cards and drew out the ace of clubs. Its pale blue design looked little different from the rest of the deck's, except that one section appeared to be darker than the rest.

"Hold your hands out," the youngster ordered the bigger dude.

"Why?"

"We could go to jail and do it."

Slowly, reluctantly it seemed, the dude obeyed, extending his hands palm upwards. As Waco half-expected, the man's right thumb carried a significant blue stain on its ball.

"I reckon we'll take that walk right now," Waco said.

"What's the charge, deputy?" demanded a voice and the gun-salesman thrust his way through the crowd. "This's my assistant, Jube Bunch."

"You should pay him more and maybe he wouldn't need to cheat at cards."

"How do you know he's been cheating?"

"I'd say he's been 'daubing'", Waco answered and reached out a hand to pull open the left pocket of Bunch's vest from which he removed a small container. "He's got blue dye in here, puts it on his thumb and marks the cards."

"And how many has he marked so far?" asked Tomkins.

"Only the one that I've seen," Waco admitted.

"And you reckon that's enough evidence to take him in?"

"I'd say so."

"There's some might think different," Tomkins said in a carrying voice.

"There always is," Waco answered, wondering what the man was driving at.

"They might even think you're trying to make a name as a crooked gambling expert who can't be fooled."

"Why'd they do that?" Waco asked.

"So that when the inquest into young Minshull comes up everybody'll take your word that he wasn't getting cheated," the gun salesman announced, still keeping his voice raised high.

"You got the answer to why I'd do that?"

"We've heard the lawmen getting paid off to miss things afore," Tomkins replied. "Only somebody caught on he was being cheated—"

"Are you saying that's what happened here?" Waco said, his voice hardly more than a whisper.

"I'm saying that you're not railroading my assistant to cover—"

Around lashed Waco's right hand, driving its knuckles full into Tomkins's mouth. Even as the salesman staggered back, Bunch lunged at the deputy. Drawing the left side Colt, Waco laid its barrel against the dude's jaw and tumbled him to the floor. Tomkins caught his balance, raised a hand to his mouth and looked at the blood on it. Fury showed on his face as he glared at the youngster.

"You're brave enough with a gun in your hand," Tomkins spat out. "And against an unarmed man."

"Likely," Waco answered. "And you've a right smart answer to that."

"You don't scare me, deputy," Tomkins replied. "Tomorrow at nine o'clock I'm coming down the street out there and if you're still in town I'll kill you."

"I'll be there," Waco promised and nodded to the groaning Bunch. "Two of you haul him down to the jail."

"Don't worry none, Jube," Tomkins told his assistant. "Comes nine o'clock tomorrow you'll be walking out of that jail without a stain on your character."

Talk welled up after the main participants in the drama left the saloon. Only one topic interested the customers and staff alike. Could a dude face up to and survive against the blond youngster's chain-lightning fast draw?

One person appeared to think so.

"I saw that salesman shoot and the deputy didn't dare stack against him," the small card-player said. "And I'm willing to bet three to one that he gets the deputy in the morning."

"I'll take some of that," a man said. "Will you go as high as twenty bucks, mister—"

"I'll go as high as anybody wants to bet," replied the man. "And the name is Ross."

Feed thudded on the sidewalk outside the jail as Waco sat at the desk and wrote in the log. He heard voices and could tell what incident the passers-by discussed.

"I'll tell you that dude's a heap better shot than the deputy," said one of the passing men. "He proved that today."

Waco had also been considering that point.

Glancing at the wall clock, which showed the time to be almost nine, Waco slipped his right hand Colt into the holster. Outside the street lay as empty and devoid of life as the bottom of Death Valley on a hot summer afternoon; except for the small nondescript man who stood on the opposite sidewalk and darted glances around him. However behind every window and inside each partly opened door eyes watched and waited for the first sign that Tomkins aimed to keep his threat. Across the office, the old jailer peered through the window and turned in Waco's direction.

"He's coming."

"I figured he would," the youngster drawled and walked from the room.

There could be no avoiding the challenge. If Waco did so, he would be unable to continue wearing the deputy's badge.

Which did not matter much as he would be riding back to the OD Connected after the trial, or on the sheriff's return. However his refusal might do untold harm, make trouble for the other peace officers of the area; and he refused to allow it to happen.

As Waco stepped through the door, he saw the man across the street take out a large bandana handkerchief and dab upwards as if to wipe off sweat. Then the youngster located Tomkins. The salesman stood in the center of the street a good sixty yards away.

"You turning him loose deputy?" Tomkins yelled.

"No!" Waco called back, but thoughts raced through his head.

Without advancing, Tomkins dropped his hand to slide the Smith & Wesson out of its holster. The move was not exceptionally fast; nor did it need to be at such a distance. Bringing out the revolver, Tomkins began to turn into the fancy target-shooting position he used so effectively on the previous day.

Acting on instinct, Waco started to reach for his right-side Colt. Even as the gun cleared leather, he analyzed the situation and recognized the danger. At fifty yards the Peacemaker could not be relied on for accurate work; nor had it been designed with that kind of use in mind. Simple of mechanism, rugged and dependable, hard-hitting and carrying a butt which lent itself to instinctive-alignment pointing the Peacemaker had no peer as a close-range fighting weapon. Fifty yards was anything but close range.

Already the other man lined his Smith & Wesson and Waco flung himself aside. Nor did the youngster move a moment too soon. He saw flame lick from the Smith & Wesson's barrel, then heard the sound of a close-passing bullet which must have caught him in the head if he had stood still.

Going down in a rolling dive, Waco landed on the ground where the sidewalk ended between the sheriff's office and next building. He started to rise, meaning to rest his wrists on the sidewalk and use a double-handed hold while aiming at Tomkins. Then he recalled a detail which saved his life. When passing on the warning, Sammy claimed three men to be involved in an attempt on Waco's life. This could be the attempt. Tomkins forced a fight on flimsy grounds and took an advantage which only just bordered on what the West regarded as fair dealing. With Bunch in jail and Tomkins along the street, there remained one more man to be accounted for. From Sammy's words, the third man had been one of the plot, not the killers' employer. So he ought to be somewhere close at hand—

At which point the youngster remembered the small man who stood across from the office. Everything fell neatly into place. The trouble at the saloon, staged to provide a reason for Tomkins's challenge, could easily have taken a dangerous turn if Bunch picked on the wrong man to cheat at cards. Of course that little jasper might be no more than an innocent bystander—but Waco knew another man who appeared to be harmless and insignificant at first glance.

Twisting his head, Waco saw that the little man advanced across the street, and finding himself discovered, sent a hand flashing under his jacket. Out came a Merwin & Hulbert Army Pocket revolver in a flickering move of deadly speed and Ross threw a shot at Waco. Once more the young-

ster's lightning fast reactions saved him. Rolling over, Waco
ignored Ross's bullet which drove into the dirt at his side
and fired while lying on his back. Awkward though such a
position might be, the youngster shot with deadly effect.
Ross jerked backwards as the bullet struck him and his gun
dropped from his hand. Completing his roll, Waco saw the
little man go down and rose to his feet at the edge of the
building and looked for his other attacker.

Still Ross had not advanced along the street. Seeing Waco
rise, he lined his revolver and touched off another shot. The
wall at Waco's side erupted splinters and he felt them striking him. Momentarily blinded by pain, the youngster gave
a cry and staggered into the alley. Doing so put him out of
Tomkins's sight and prevented the man from shooting again.
Blood ran from where a splinter carved a nick over Waco's
left eye, half-blinding him but he knew the danger had not
ended.

Turning, Waco ran along the alley and around the rear
of the building. Then he darted along in Tomkins's direction
and kept the business premises between them. With his left
hand, the youngster wiped away the blood. Relief bit into
him as he discovered he could see through the eye, then
once more blood obscured his vision.

Three buildings fell behind Waco and he turned to pass
through the next alley. Coming on to the street, he found
himself facing Tomkins—only at a much shorter distance
than he had hoped for. No longer did the man stand sixty
yards away, in fact less than thirty feet separated them.

When Tomkins saw Waco reel back, he felt sure that his
bullet had taken effect. So he advanced along the street,
wanting to learn how badly Ross might be hurt then release
Bunch from the jail. While Tomkins still held his Smith &
Wesson, he never expected to use it.

Finding Waco, alive if bloody, suddenly before him

caused Tomkins to halt and raise the revolver. At longer ranges, aimed deliberately using its sights, the Smith & Wesson might be the better gun; but it never saw the day when its saw-handle butt allowed it to point as naturally as did the hand-fitting grip of the Peacemaker.

Waco skidded to a stop, going immediately into the gun-fighter's crouch and firing with his Colt held waist high. A hole appeared in the center of Tomkins's forehead. Letting the revolver fall from his fingers, the man spun around and landed face down on the street. His hat had jerked off when the bullet struck and the back of his head made a hideous sight where the colt's bullet burst out.

People began to appear at doors and the old jailer dashed out of the office. Slowly Waco wiped the blood once more from his forehead and then started to reload his Colt.

"He get you bad, Waco?" asked the jailer.

"Just nicked me's all," the youngster answered. "I've got things to do."

"Leave me tend to this pair then," grunted the deputy, knowing what Waco meant. "Is it like you figured?"

"I reckon so," Waco replied and holstered the replenished Colt as he walked towards the hotel.

A startled-looking clerk stared at Waco as the youngster demanded to know the number of Minshull's room.

"He's in the best suite, first right at the head of the stairs," the clerk replied. "But he's got somebody with him."

"He'll see me," Waco stated and went upstairs.

On reaching the first door, Waco saw Duprez about to leave Minshull's room. Giving a startled yelp, the bank manager jerked back into the room and started to slam the door. Waco sprang forward, drawing his right hand Colt. Dropping his shoulder, the youngster hit the door with all his power. A howl of dismay rose as the door burst inwards and flung Duprez across the room. Bursting in, Waco saw

Logan cowering against the wall, Duprez falling over backwards. Minshull at the table and Herbert hovering behind his employer. At the window Firwood's head disappeared out of sight as he slid down to the ground, using a rope supplied to the room as a means of escape in case of fire.

"You should've got out faster," the youngster remarked to Duprez and Logan. "I'd not thought of you pair and Firwood when I tried to figure out who'd hired that bunch to kill me."

"But you thought that I had?" asked Minshull.

"You'd cause to hate me. Only I couldn't figure out how you'd got them here so quick to do it."

"He told us we had to do it!" Logan screeched.

"That's a lie," Minshull said calmly.

"We didn't know that Firwood hired them to kill you, deputy!" Duprez yelled. "Minshull said he'd only help us if we cleared his son's name."

"And you figured to do it by making out that the dealer cheated," Waco guessed. "That tells me all I need to know."

"So you have it all figured out, deputy?" Minshull asked.

"There's only one way they could clear your son," Waco answered. "By proving he'd been cheated and maybe even getting folks to believe I shot him down without good cause. Only neither could be done with me alive."

"Good thinking," commented Minshull.

"The rest's easy. I reckon Firwood brought in the hired guns as backing if Nodern started pushing him, only Doc and me saved him needing them for that."

"Ross, the little one, made the plan!" Logan put in. "We didn't know a thing about it—"

"I'll bet you didn't," drawled Waco. "Reckon I'd best tell you, with you not knowing and all. Tomkins showed how well he could shoot, getting me ready for it. When he called me out, I'd remembered how good he shot and either run, or be scared and make a mistake. That business at the saloon was to make it look like I didn't know so much about crooked gambling as I allow to. Sure Bunch marked the one card, but it'd take a helluva lot of proving in court."

"When you found the dye he used?" asked Minshull.

"That was a vest-pocket ink-pot, clerks and business men often tote them. Only I didn't learn it until I got back to the office and took a look. After I'd run, or been killed, everything'd've been set for proving the feller didn't cheat. From then they'd've made it look like your son shot a crooked gambler and could've maybe cleared his name by lies."

"We had to do it to get Minshull's backing, deputy," Duprez groaned. "With his money, we can recover from the losses caused by Hancox and Nodern's embezzlement."

"You don't need outside help for that," Waco told the bank manager. "Texas was bust worst than this town after the War and we hauled ourselves up by the bootstraps without squealing for anybody to help us." His eyes, cold and contemptuous, raked the two men before him. "All you need is the guts to try."

"What do you aim to do to us?" Duprez asked.

"That depends on you. I'm willing to do nothing, happen you get the hell out of here and stand on your own feet, without his help."

"Just a minute—" Minshull began, shoving back his chair and starting to rise.

"It's your choice," Waco went on without giving a sign that he heard the interruption. "Take his backing, if he'll give it, and you're his body and soul. He won't just use you as partners, you'll be his slaves."

Which just about matched the uneasy suspicion Duprez had been forming ever since first listening to Minshull's conditions for support. Cold rage swept over the financier's face as he read the decision Duprez and Logan reached even before they put it to words.

"Get him, Herbert!" Minshull shouted, rising and sending his chair flying.

Instead of leaping forward to obey the order, Herbert shook his head. "Not me, boss, I'se seed that boy shoot."

"Damn you!" the financier bellowed and lashed a savage backhand blow across Herbert's face.

Herbert staggered, caught his balance and snarled like an enraged animal. Sending his hand under the jacket to where his razor lay concealed, he started to move towards his employer.

"Hold it!" Waco ordered, lining his Colt on Herbert. "If you try to kill him I'll have to decide whether to stop you and I'd hate like hell to have to make *that* decision."

Slowly Herbert removed his hand from the razor. Then he turned and walked out of the room. Duprez exchanged a long glance with Logan before facing Minshull.

"We'll make do without you," the bank manager said.

"The price would be too high," Logan went on.

After the two men left, Minshull studied the tall, blond youngster.

"All the money I spent sending him to good schools and hiring fancy teachers, deputy," the man said. "And what did I get? A drunken, stupid, incompetent no-account with the brains of a louse and the morals of an alley-cat."

"He was your son," Waco pointed out.

"And yet you, a boy years younger than him, you can hold down a responsible post like deputy sheriff," Minshull went on as if he had not heard a word the other said. "You're all Jervis never was. Smart, capable, tough when there's need for it. I don't know whether I hated or admired you more."

"You tried to get me killed."

"I didn't hire those—"

"Nope, you didn't," interrupted Waco. "But you knew the only way those three jaspers could do what you asked would be after I was dead."

"You came through it, though," Minshull said.

"And two men died. There's a stage out tonight. Be on it and keep going until you're clear of Texas."

"If I don't?" demanded the financier.

"I'll see that word gets around about what you pulled here. Maybe I can't do it myself, but my boss, Ole Devil Hardin, can."

Although he hated to even think it, Minshull knew Waco told the truth. Not even a man as wealthy as Minshull could cross Ole Devil Hardin with impunity and the financier believed in steering clear of powerful enemies if he could.

"Why don't you come with me?" he asked, watching Waco's face. "I'll let you be the son I always wanted. You'll have everything you want—"

"I've got just about all I want right now," Waco interrupted.

"But everything I have would be yours in the end. I'd teach you business and with your ability, you'd stand a chance of becoming the richest man in the whole United States."

"No thanks, Mr. Minshull," Waco replied. "I might wind up thinking and acting like you—and I'd hate like hell to do that."

PART FIVE

A Case of Infectious "Plumbeus Veneficium"

There were, Doc Leroy admitted to himself, disadvantages to possessing a knowledge of medicine. Returning to the OD Connected with Red Blaze and Waco after hunting down and killing the murderer of Sunshine Sam Catlan.* Doc insisted the trio called in to visit his uncle, a medical man in Mound Prairie. They could hardly have picked a better time to arrive, for Doctor Hamish Lamming had finally persuaded his very efficient housekeeper to become his wife and the wedding would take place the following morning.

No bachelor of Lamming's standing could be permitted to embark in matrimony without all his male friends giving him a rousing send-off and the three young cowhands found Mound Prairie to be preparing for a night of celebrations long to be remembered. Never averse to joining such an event, Doc, Red and Waco eagerly accepted Lamming and the bride-to-be's invitation to stay over until after the ceremony.

Everything seemed set for the trio to settle down and forget the hectic time spent in Hood City as they hunted for

* Told in *Waco's Debt*.

the murderer of Waco's foster-father. Then word reached the saloon that Doctor Lamming's services were required. It seemed that little Willie Gelder climbed a tree after a baby raccoon and fell down again, so required medical attention. Doc knew that his uncle found little time to relax completely, being the only doctor in Anderson County, and so offered to answer the call for Lamming. At first Lamming objected, then reluctantly agreed, with the proviso that Doc sent word should the boy's condition prove too serious.

Surprise came to Mrs. Gelder's plump face when the door to Lamming's office opened and a tall, slim young cowhand entered instead of the familiar figure of the town's liked and respected doctor. At first she thought the newcomer might be in need of medical aid, but he removed his Stetson and hung it on the hatrack horns of a bull elk by the door. Next Doc peeled off his jacket, its right side stitched back to leave clear access to the ivory-handled Colt Civilian Peacemaker riding in the contoured holster of his well-made gunbelt about his waist. The belt came off after Doc had hung his coat alongside the Stetson. It was a significant rig to eyes which knew of such matters, telling its owner was a man highly-skilled in gunfighting ways. Doc placed the belt on the rack, which also held a hat and jacket belonging to his uncle, then turned to the woman.

"What's wrong with the boy?" he asked.

"I sent for the doctor," Mrs. Gelder yelped.

"He asked me to come along and handle things for him, ma'am."

Studying Doc's pale face—it had a tan-resisting skin which never bronzed in the sun—she saw no hint that the visit might be cowhand horse-play. Clearly the newcomer spoke the truth. Which meant that, no matter how he dressed, the young man must be capable of attending to her son. Doctor Lamming would never have sent him otherwise. She wondered why a doctor should use to dress as a cowhand, but asked no questions.

Which was fortunate for her peace of mind.

While Doc Leroy had handled medical and surgical work on numerous occasions, he was not a qualified doctor. Financial and family troubles prevented him from spending more than a year in a St. Louis medical college and on his return to a Texas struggling to recover from the Civil War he, like most other youngsters, turned to cattle for a living. After learning his trade, Doc became a member of the Wedge, an outfit which contracted to deliver cattle to the Kansas market for ranchers unable to make the long drive north themselves.

In addition to becoming a master hand with cattle, Doc continued his medical studies. He read every book that came his way, spent time with doctors in any town his work led him to, and put his knowledge to practical use. In addition to mending broken bones, he dealt with such diseases as he could among the trail crew and four babies came into the world due to his presence and ability. He also extracted bullets; so much so that he probably knew more about that branch of medical science than many highly qualified surgeons of international repute who lived in the more sheltered East.

With the ever-advancing railroads approaching Texas, the great interstate trail drives would no longer be necessary and so Stone Hart, boss of the Wedge, decided the time had come to buy a ranch and settle down. Although Doc meant to go with his boss to Arizona, family affairs held him in Texas. Needing work, he accepted Dusty Fog's offer to join the OD Connected and rode with the floating outfit.

He could claim to be equal to any member of that hard-riding bunch in the swift and accurate use of a Colt Peacemaker when the need arose.

Knowing none of that, Mrs. Gelder accepted Doc as Lamming's *locum tenens* and if she thought about his cow-hand clothes put them down to being donned in fun as part of Lamming's party celebrations.

"Willie fell down a tree late this afternoon. At first I thought nothing of it. He walked home and didn't seem to have more than a few bruises. Then this evening he began to complain of pains in his chest."

"Did, huh?" Doc said, studying the youngster. "Hasn't anybody ever told you it's a fool way to come down a tree."

"Huh?" said the youngster.

"The same way you went up it, boy," Doc drawled as he unfastened his bandana and draped it over his hat. "Head first."

Although the boy tried to smile, he did not make a very good job of it. He sat on the hard horse-hair couch and kept his breathing shallow as that way hurt less. However he had no wish for the new doctor to regard him as a sissy and so bore a stoical expression on his tear-stained face.

"Arms and legs working all right, boy?" Doc asked.

"Sure," Willie answered.

"We'd best take a look at your chest then."

"I tried to get his shirt off, doctor," the woman put in. "The pain was too much for him to stand."

"It'll have to come off though," Doc insisted. "Can I cut it off?"

"Of course."

Taking a pair of scissors from the instrument cupboard in the corner of the room, Doc returned to the couch and grinned at Willie's suddenly scared expression.

"Mind one time I had to do this for Dusty Fog," Doc drawled.

Interest showed on the boy's face. "Do you know Dusty Fog?"

"My home's in the Rio Hondo," Doc replied. "Fact being, I came in today with Waco and Red Blaze."

"Gee!" Willie gasped. "I'd sure like to meet them."

"Tell you then," Doc said. "Tomorrow I'll have 'em come 'round and visit if your mammy'll let 'em."

"Of course they can," smiled Mrs. Gelder, watching Doc slit down the front of the shirt while holding the boy's attention.

"What'd Cap'n Fog done?" asked Willie, ignoring the pain caused as Doc began to remove the shirt in the manner of taking off a jacket.

"Got piled off a hoss," improvised Doc. "He landed a mite awkward, let me fix him up and then go back on and rid that old hoss to a standstill."

"He would," breathed Willie, hero-worship showing plain on his face.

"Which same don't mean that you've got to go and climb that tree again to prove you can," warned Doc, starting to examine the boy's chest. "That hoss had to be ridden so it could go into the remuda. Dusty didn't just do it to show how tough he is."

Hoping that the moral of the story sank home. Doc looked at the boy's right side. Considerable bruising showed, but Willie gave no signs of internal hemorrhage which would mean the broken ends of the rib bones had been driven inwards and damaged the lungs or other organs. Gently Doc ran his fingers over the bruised area.

"Hurt?" he asked.

"No—" Willie said.

"Now looky here, boy," Doc growled, straightening up. "You don't have to lie to prove how tough you are. If it hurts, say so and if I hurt you, yell out. Mind one time we was out hunting and the Ysabel Kid got a porcupine quill stuck in his leg. He howled fit to bust a man's ears when I hauled it out again."

"H—The Kid yelled?"

"Can't think of a better way to tell a man you're being hurt," Doc replied and resumed his examination.

Touching gently at the bruising once more, Doc detected an irregularity of the skin surface and also felt crepitus, the grating of the fractured ends of the bones. This time Willie did not hold down his gasp of pain and Doc immediately halted his search.

"Works better that way, doesn't it, boy?" he asked and Willie nodded.

"How bad is it, doctor?" Mrs. Gelder asked worriedly.

"Couple of ribs cracked, but not badly," Doc replied. "I'll strap them up for him and you can bring him in to see Uncle Hamish tomorrow afternoon."

Working with smooth, practiced ease, Doc wound wide bandages around the injured area. He made Willie breath out so as to empty the chest before securing the bandages and when he stepped back knew that he had done a good job. Glancing at Mrs. Gelder, he grinned and then asked how Willie felt.

"Better," the boy replied. "You won't forget about tomorrow."

"I'll have 'em along to see you sure as shooting," Doc replied.

"Can I pay you, doctor?" Mrs. Gelder inquired.

"See Uncle Hamish about it, ma'am."

"Well I brought along a blueberry pie for Hamish," the woman said, nodding to a basket by the door. "You must have that."

"Way I like blueberry pie, you'll hear no argument, ma'am," Doc assured her.

The pie looked exceptionally inviting, thick, well-filled and topped over by a golden brown crust. If it could be faulted, one might say it was a touch small to be shared among the guests at Lamming's bachelor party; all of whom probably possessed a well-developed taste for such a delicacy.

"Where shall I put it?" the woman asked.

"On the table there, by Uncle Hamish's bag."

"Watch you don't crack it and get the juice on anything. It stains something awful."

"I'll tend to it, ma'am," Doc promised.

After Mrs. Gelder and Willie left the room, Doc washed his hands and packed away the bandages he had not used. Footsteps sounded outside, made by high heeled range boots, or Doc missed his guess. As Anderson County lay a mite east of the main cattle country, it saw few cowhands. So probably Waco and Red approached. Doc's eyes went to the pie. It sure did seem a shame to share that pie with a dozen or so hungry jaspers, especially as none of them did a lick of work to deserve any. With that understandable, if unworthy, thought in mind, Doc looked around for a means of concealing his spoils. There would be no time to go far, nor the need. Taking up the pie, he placed it into his uncle's open but empty medical bag. Then, assuming an air of bland innocence, he turned towards the opening door.

Although the two men who entered each topped the six foot mark and wore range clothing, Doc needed only one glance to tell they were not his friends. Which did not mean Doc failed to recognize them. Unless he missed his guess, the bearded jasper at the right would be Kag Bowery. The hooknosed, mean-looking cuss at Bowery's side bore the name Charley Dorris on the last wanted dodger Doc remembered seeing of him.

"What the hell?" Doc growled.

"No fuss there, Doc," warned Bowery, drawing his Colt.

"We've done brought you some business," Dorris went on.

"We sure have," Bowery agreed. "Get your gear together, Doc, we've a mighty sick feller for you."

"Bring him in here," Doc suggested, certain the men did not recognize him and used the name as they would to any doctor.

"Ain't at all possible, Doc," Bowery replied. "See, he's got him a bullet in his chest and don't look too good at all."

"Seeing's how he knows something we have to know, we want him alive," Dorris explained. "Now are you coming, or do we have to beat you over the head a mite to make you?"

Doc directed a glance at his gunbelt. If he could only reach it, things would rapidly take a change for the better. Before the chance came, Dorris also saw the belt and let out an appreciative grunt. Stepping to the rack, he lifted down the belt and examined its workmanship.

"Whooee!" he said, drawing the Colt and hefting it before testing the smooth way it cocked. "Whoever owned this outfit knew what he was about. The gun comes out as smooth as silk and its works've been doctored up just right. Who owns it, Doc?"

"Some gun-slick I tried to patch up after he run in with our marshal," Doc replied. "He died and I kept the gunbelt to sell to cover my working fee."

"Sure hope you have better luck with Cosby," Bowery grunted. "Take the damned thing if you want it, Charley, and let's get going."

"You coming along, Doc?" grinned Dorris, hanging the gunbelt over his shoulder.

"Do I have any choice?"

"Not happen you want to keep on living."

"Then I'll come along peaceable. Let me pack my bag."

"Go to it," ordered Bowery, scratching at his beard with his left hand.

While collecting the necessary implements for removing a bullet and treating its wound, Doc watched for some chance to reverse his position. None came. Maybe the two men did not rank as high up the outlaw social scale as Sam Bass, but they acted proficient enough to make taking rash chances decidedly dangerous. After packing the bag, Doc walked across to the door.

"Get your hat and coat, Doc," Bowery growled. "Happen somebody saw you going riding without 'em, they might think something's wrong."

Doc turned to the rack and started to reach for his hat. Then an idea struck him. When he did not return to the party, his friends were sure to come looking for him. If they found him gone, but his hat and coat still in the room, they would guess he did not leave on his own free will. Fortunately he and Lamming stood about the same height and build, so he could wear the doctor's clothes without arousing his captor's suspicions.

"You got anything for a pain in the guts, Doc?" Dorris inquired, twisting his face in a grimace of pain.

"Sure, I can—"

"Forget it!" snapped Bowery. "We've got to get moving."

With that he opened the door and peered cautiously out. Seeing nothing to disturb him, he signalled for Doc to leave. Being wise in such matters, Doc played safe and obeyed his captors. When the time came, he could make his move and until then might as well lull their suspicions by acting in a complaisant manner.

Alert for any chance, Doc accompanied the men to where

three horses stood fastened to the picket fence at the rear of the building. Bowery told him to take the center animal and he went to obey. Clearly he dealt with men who knew their business for the reins of Doc's mount had been fastened to the horses on either side of it instead of to the fence. He mounted and the two men swung into their saddles. Not until sure of their position did they unfasten his reins and start moving.

Waco and Red Blaze saw the three riders go by as they approached the doctor's house in search of Doc. More than that, they recognized their friend. Even as Red opened his mouth to call out, he realized that Doc did not ride as a free agent.

"Trouble, Waco," Red hissed.

"Sure. Doc'd not be wearing those clothes or letting that jasper tote his gun if he didn't have to."

A tall, well-made man a few years older than Waco, Red had a mop of fiery hair and a freckled, pugnaciously handsome face made for grinning. He wore range clothes, with a multihued silk bandana knotted at his throat. About his waist hung a gunbelt supporting walnut Colt Cavalry Peacemakers butt forward in low cavalry-draw holsters. While Red might have a penchant for becoming involved in trouble and a habit for pitching into any fight he found without troubling to learn its cause, he acted cool and steady enough when necessary. So he did not go off half-cocked when seeing a good friend in danger.

"We can't chance shooting from here," he said.

"That's for sure," Waco agreed. "Best get the hosses and see if we can catch up to them."

Both knew they stood little chance of following the men by reading sign, but they intended to make a damned good try.

* * *

Holding their horses to a fast trot, Bowery and Dorris herded Doc across the range country in a south-westerly direction. While riding, Doc thought over what he knew about his captors. The name Cosby dropped by Bowery told Doc enough to warn him his chances of survival had seldom been worse. Among Texas outlaws, Wade Cosby stood high on the tree. A bank robbery by preference, Cosby planned well, made big hauls and showed no concern over taking human life. Nobody falling into Cosby's hands could look upon it with ease and Doc knew he would need all his skill, plus a whole heap of luck, to come out of the affair alive.

No chance of escaping presented itself and they covered almost five miles with the silence only relieved when Dorris complained of his aching stomach. At last they drew near to a small cabin which lay at the bottom of a fold of land. Only three horses stood in the corral and there did not appear to be any guard out. However, on Bowery giving a shrill whistle, a light glowed at one window and the door opened to allow a Winchester's barrel to poke out.

"That you, Bowery?" barked a voice from behind the rifle.

"You're expecting maybe General Grant?" Bowery answered, scratching at his beard as he had done several times during the ride.

Leaving the horses at the corral, Bowery and Dorris followed Doc towards the cabin's door. It seemed that neither man intended leaving the other with Doc for some reason, as they did not even wait to tend to their mounts. On their approach, the door opened and a stocky, middle-sized man looked out. Doc figured he would be Jess Taunton, Cosby's right hand man; as mean as a stick-teased rattlesnake and deadlier than a cottonmouth moccasin.

"This is the doctor?" Taunton asked.

"Sure," Bowery replied. "How's Wade?"

"About the same. Still unconscious. Come on over here, Doc and take a look at him."

The cabin proved to be of the small, one-room variety thrown up to house a small family. Apart from Taunton, the room appeared to be empty. Then Doc saw a blanket-covered shape on one of the four bunks which lined the walls. Food and a couple of whisky bottles stood on the table in the center of the room and four chairs around it formed the last of the cabin's furnishings. Following Taunton, Doc haulted by the bunk and set his bag on its end.

"What happened?" he asked.

"There's been some fuss," Taunton answered. "I want him saving and getting well enough to talk."

After looking down at a lean, haggard, pain-twisted and sweat-dappled face for a moment, Doc drew back the blanket. He found Cosby to still be dressed and a bloody rag was pressed on to the man's chest.

"All right," Doc snapped, taking the injured man's right wrist between his thumb and forefinger. "I want something rigging around here. Make a screen out of blankets—"

"Why?" growled Taunton.

"Because I say so. I'm not working with your bunch looking on."

"You giving us orders?" Bowery spat out.

"If you want Cosby alive I am," Doc agreed. "Mister, he's near to gone and there's no other doctor within a day's ride—"

"Do what he wants, boys," ordered Taunton, in the bitter tone of one who knows the opposition holds all the cards.

Ignoring the two men as they started to fix up ropes which would support the screening blankets, Doc took the man's pulse and found it to be very weak. Then he removed the rag and looked down at the wound.

"Did the bullet go right through?" he asked.

"No," Taunton answered.

"How'd it happen and what'd he get hit with?"

"We were playing poker and Miguel Ramon couldn't agree with Wade over who should hold the king of hearts. Ole Wade's not as fast as he used to be, or Mig'd never got that Derringer out."

"Where's the other feller?"

"Wade might be slowing, but not that much. Mig's out in the barn. He don't mind it one lil bit."

"You figure he'll live?" Dorris inquired, hanging a blanket over the ropes.

"I'm a pretty fair doctor, but I'm not a Comanche medicine woman," Doc replied, casting an envious glance to where his gunbelt and Colt lay on the man's bunk. "So I can't see into the future. One thing I do know, sooner I'm started, the better his chances."

Taking the hint, Taunton growled for his companions to get on with their work. By the time they finished, Doc stood with his patient inside a cubicle made of blankets and hidden from view of the three men.

"No tricks, mind, Doc," warned Taunton.

"Against three of you and all armed?" Doc spat back. "Now get the hell away from me and stay there."

Much to his surprise, the outlaw obeyed. As he opened up the medical bag, Doc wondered what caused the trio to be so interested in saving their boss's life. No matter how well Doc worked, Cosby would be bedridden for a fair length of time and his men could hardly stay in such a location without attracting attention. However there would be time to worry about motives later. First he had a serious and delicate doctoring chore on his hands.

The pulse-beat told Doc his patient was in a weak condition, but he doubted if any pain caused by removing the bullet would pierce through the blanket of unconsciousness which enfolded the outlaw. Taking up a long, thin probe, Doc inserted its end into the hole and began to feel delicately for the bullet. At last his fingers detected the piece of lead and he paused, studying in his mind's eye the layout of the chest and position of the vital organs.

"Why the hell didn't you learn something useful, like school teaching?" he asked himself silently as he realized the serious nature of the task ahead.

Withdrawing the probe, Doc replaced it by a specially designed set of long, thin forceps. He threw a look at the blankets, heard the men talking beyond them and turned back to his work.

"He's sure taking his time," Dorris muttered restlessly, sitting at the table with Doc's gunbelt and Colt before him.

"I don't give a damn as long as he gets Wade well enough to tell us where he stashed away the money," Taunton replied. "Say, that's a real good gunbelt."

"Yeah. I'll have to alter it some before it rides right though."

Silence fell once more and the men sat around the table with eyes continually darting at the blankets. Time dragged by and at last the blankets jerked aside. One look at Doc's face brought all the men to their feet.

"If he's de—!" Taunton began.

"Damn it!" Doc interrupted. "You fools never told me that he had infectious *Plumbeus Veneficium.*"

While none of the trio had any idea what Doc meant, they all understood one word, "infectious". From the expression on the doctor's face, that fancy-sounding illness must be real dangerous.

"What in hell's that?" Taunton asked, putting his companions' thoughts into words.

"Infectious *Plumbeus Veneficium,*" Doc answered in a

hushed voice. "Look here at him, man."

Jerking aside and throwing down the blankets, the three men gathered about their wounded leader's bunk. While they could see that he still lived and looked a mite easier, his chest swathed in bandages, none paid much attention to it. Instead they stared at his lips which had turned a shade deep blue.

"It—It's like he'd been eating blueberry pie," Dorris gasped.

"And had he?" Doc asked.

"We've been on sour-belly and beans for a week," Taunton answered.

"Then it's infectious *Plumbeus Veneficium* for sure," Doc stated. "The blue lips are one sign. Another is pains in the stomach—"

"I've got pains in my guts," Dorris announced in a scared voice.

"And another sign's the jaws feel all itchy, you have to keep scratching them," Doc went on, edging towards the table.

Although Bowery's scared expression mirrored that of Dorris, Taunton remained unimpressed.

"Huh. I'm been 'round him all day and I never felt better."

"Lord!" gasped Doc. "That's the worst sign of all. Last feller I knew who caught it was as healthy as they come. Moved fast and just dropped down dead."

Concern flickered for a moment on Taunton's face and he directed a glance at the still shape on the bed. If Taunton fought against his fears of the unknown disease, the same did not apply to his companions.

"You've got to do something for us, Doc!" Bowery yelled, staring at Cosby's blue lips with fascinated horror.

"Here's your bag!" Dorris went on, reaching for it.

Self-interest formed a large part of all the trio's make-up. Each one wanted to be the first to receive whatever aid the doctor might be able to give. So Bowery also grabbed for the bag and Taunton, affected by his companions' fear, also moved closer. None of them looked at Doc and he continued his cautious approach to the table.

"Hey!" Dorris suddenly yelped. "There's a blueberry pie in here."

A fact which Taunton and Bowery had become aware of at almost the same moment. More significant than the mere presence of the pie, to Taunton's way of thinking, was a hole in its crust as if somebody inserted two fingers into the fruit below.

"It's a trick!" Taunton yelled and started to turn, hand dropping to his gun.

Doc had hoped to reach the table and appropriate his Colt before the men discovered the deception. Only a slow, silent and cautious advance would no longer do it. Even as Taunton looked into the bag, Doc hurled himself forward. Landing on the top of the table, Doc closed his fingers around the ivory handle of his Colt and could not remember a time when the gun felt so good to him. Continuing his roll, he gave the Colt a jerk which slid it free of the holster and tossed the gunbelt to one side.

Flame ripped from the barrel of Taunton's Colt and the concussion of the shot seemed to fill the room. The bullet stirred Doc's hair as he went over the edge of the table and fell to the floor. On landing, he took the brief split-second necessary to aim and squeezed the trigger. As his Colt bucked high with the recoil, Doc knew he aimed true. Against a man of Taunton's speed there could be only one answer and Doc shot to kill. Coming up, the .45 bullet struck under Taunton's nose and ranged on to burst out at the top rear of his skull. Taunton jerked backwards, legs striking the end of the bed over which he fell and landed on the floor.

Already Bowery had come out of his state of surprise and his hand fanned to the waiting gun's butt. From finishing Taunton, Doc turned the Colt and drove his second bullet into Bowery's thigh. A screech burst from the bearded man's lips as his leg buckled under him and he fell. In falling, fortunately for him, he dropped his gun. Doc learned peace officer work under Dusty Fog and fully understood the prime rule of shooting again if the other man looked like continuing the fight.

A sickening realization bit into Dorris as the guns began to roar. His hand dipped to close on pants leg instead of a weapon. While trying on Doc's gunbelt, Dorris had been compelled to remove his own. Much to his horror, he saw the belt draped across his bunk and with the width of the room between them. Even as he started to move in the belt's direction, he heard Doc shoot again and a screech of agony bursting from Bowery.

"Hold it, *hombre!*" Doc ordered.

There was a certain significant smoothness in the way the "doctor" changed his aim, cocking the Colt on its recoil with the minimum of effort or delay, and lined its barrel on Dorris. To the outlaw's mind it spelled a man supremely expert in the *pistolero* art. Disobeying one so efficient would prove mighty dangerous, unless—

Face twisted in pain, Bowery still forced himself to reach towards his fallen revolver. Catching the expression on Dorris's face, Doc flickered a quick glance at the other outlaw and saw his danger. As soon as Bowery reached the gun's butt, Dorris aimed to dive for the bed—and Doc could not stop one fast enough to prevent the other killing him.

Hooves thundered, drawing rapidly closer to the cabin. Doc wondered if other members of the gang approached. However a look at the despairing expression which twisted

Dorris's face led him to believe the other did not expect aid from the approaching riders.

"Doc!" yelled a familiar voice. "You all right, Doc?"

"Get him!" Bowery yelled and grabbed for the gun.

At the same moment Dorris hurled himself in the direction of his bunk. Doc swung his Colt and fired at the more immediate danger, sending his bullet at Bowery. Outside the hooves came so close that it seemed the horses would crash into the cabin. Flying lead struck the floor by Bowery's hand and caused him to jerk it away from the gun in an involuntary gesture. However Doc knew that he could not prevent Dorris reaching the bunk.

With a shattering crash, the door burst open. Guns in hand, Red Blaze and Waco hurtled into the cabin. Pivoting around, Red shot Dorris even as the man's hand closed on the butt of his gun. Although only hit high in the shoulder, Dorris lost all inclination to fight. So did Bowery, wriggling away from his gun as well as he could to show his pacific intentions.

"What kept you," asked Doc, coming to his feet.

"Waal, there was this cute lil red-headed gal—" Red began.

"And you a married man, for shame," Doc scoffed. "What'll Sue have to say?"

Another man entered. He wore a marshal's badge and Doc knew him to be the head of Mound City's law enforcement body.

"Huh!" the marshall grunted, looking around. We could've stayed at Hamish's party, he didn't need us.

"He always is an awkward cuss when he's working," Waco replied.

"Which same I've got to start work again, damn it," growled Doc, looking at the two wounded outlaws.

"How'd you pair come at the right time like that?" Doc

asked, washing his hands after finishing patching up the outlaws' wounds and telling of his own side of the affair.

"We saw them sneaking off with you," Red answered. "Happen there'd been a gal along we'd've thought you was eloping—"

"'Cept we knew no gal'd elope with you while I'm around," Waco went on. "So we headed back to collect our hosses and met the marshal. Time we got mounted, we couldn't hear nothing of you, only we got to figuring where they'd took you."

Doc could imagine the scene, having had experience of Waco's ability in figuring similar problems. The youngster had asked questions, learning the lay of the surrounding land. After passing up other directions on various grounds, he decided the southwest offered their best chance. On hearing of the deserted cabin, Waco suggested that it, the only available shelter in many miles, might be the place to look. Backed by Red's faith in his deductive powers, Waco persuaded the marshal to go along with him and proved to be correct.

"You ought to be ashamed of yourself, Doc," Red drawled. "Lying to those gents that-away."

"I didn't lie," Doc replied calmly.

"You mean they've got that whatever you said they had?" Waco asked.

"Sure. *Plumbeus Veneficium's* the Latin name for lead poisoning. I reckon they all wound up with it in the end."